FLAWLESS MISTAKE

THE SPENCER & SIONE SERIES – PREQUEL

FLAWLESS MISTAKE

RACHEL WOODS

BONZAI
MOON

BonzaiMoon Books LLC
Houston, Texas
www.bonzaimoonbooks.com

Editing by Kelly Hartigan of Xterra Web
http://editing.xterraweb.com

Book cover designed by Deranged Doctor Design
http://www.derangeddoctordesign.com

ISBN 978-1-943685-00-4 (Print)

Thank you Lord for your mercy, grace and love.

To my favorite sister, Angelique. Thanks for your patient endurance, tireless encouragement and willingness to read everything I put before you throughout the years.

To my favorite mother, Betty. Thanks for being a true "alpha female!"

1

He was kissing her again.

He moved his mouth over hers delicately, slowly, but commanding and insistent.

Eagerly, she opened her mouth, and he slipped his tongue between her lips. She felt his erection, and her heart slammed. His hands moved from her breasts to her neck, his fingertips like fire against her skin, his thumb pressing into her throat, and his nails digging into the back of her neck.

She gasped into his mouth, arching against him.

He moved his head back and stared at her.

His dark eyes were glazed and luminescent, hypnotizing, terrifying.

He tightened his hands around her neck.

She opened her legs, and he entered her, thrusting into her, his hands still around her throat. She couldn't breathe. She wrapped her legs around his, rocking her hips. He thrust faster, deeper into her. Trying to breathe, she bucked desperately against him, and—

Spencer Edwards sat up, heart thundering as her head whipped back and forth.

Eyes opened wide, she struggled to see in the darkened room, trying to catch her breath as the haze dissipated from her mind.

She'd been dreaming. Having a damn nightmare, she realized as her heart slowed, returning to normal. Some kind of crazy sex-and-torture nightmare.

As her gaze adjusted to the darkness, she was able to discern the shapes and shadows surrounding her as they came into focus. Bureau drawers, armoire, dresser, full-length mirror, and two love seats separated by a small coffee table.

She was in a bedroom, between the damp, twisted sheets of a king-sized bed.

And she wasn't alone.

Spencer turned her head and stared at the man lying next to her. Ben Chang.

Good-looking and sexy, he had a complexion as smooth and dark as the coffee grown in the mountains of Jamaica, his birthplace, and features that were unmistakably Asian, the Chinese ancestry dominant in the nose, cheekbones, and almond eyes.

Involuntarily, Spencer touched her throat, remembering the hands tightening around her neck in that strange nightmare.

Why the hell had she been dreaming about Ben choking her, trying to kill her as he made love to her? What the hell was that about? And what did it mean that she felt a slight ache between her legs, a sly swirling that aroused her?

Spencer glanced at Ben again, still sleeping, his back to her.

Maybe she'd dreamt about him because they'd had sex for the first time tonight.

Explosive, mind-blowing sex that took her breath away and left her dazed and trembling, yearning for more.

Since meeting Ben, Spencer had given serious thought to maybe seeing what could happen between the two of them.

But the rational, independent part of her knew that love and romance were concepts she didn't really trust, though not for the reasons most people assumed.

Spencer didn't have a string of bad break-ups to be bitter about, and there weren't any horrendous romantic disappointments to blame for her reluctance to take a chance on love.

Instead, she had the example of her mother, who regularly and willingly lost her mind over men. Being a witness to her mother's self-inflicted heartache, Spencer had decided she would not be tricked into believing she had some soul mate ready to sweep her off her feet; she would not waste her time searching and longing for love and happiness, two illusive constructs that only led to despair and destruction.

But, for some reason, Spencer had begun to feel differently about love since she'd met Ben Chang, as if she might abandon some of her old defenses.

Maybe.

The day she'd met Ben had been bright and sunny, one of those beautiful spring days, with both a trace of lingering coolness from winter and a hint of the humidity that would soon blanket the city.

She remembered thinking it was too pretty a day to be so frustrated and sad. And yet there she was, sitting on a park bench in front of the reflecting pool at City Hall, trying to figure out how the hell she'd blown the job interview she'd had earlier that morning.

After her disastrous interview, she'd left the glass and chrome skyscraper and walked out into piercing sunshine, feeling as though she didn't even matter, convinced that nothing good would ever happen to her, and she would have to continue manipulating and deceiving men to make ends meet.

Although, the phrase "manipulating and deceiving" was a bit rude, a little too real, too mercenary and shameful.

The preferred term was "dating," according to her older half-sister, Desarae Bedard, who had designed the repugnant scheme after falling on hard times.

As explained by Rae, "dating" was a creative way to pay the bills, to put food on the table, and keep a roof over your head.

Scamming dirty old men out of their luxury goods had been Rae's "profession" for the past year and a half, and she'd pretty much mastered the art of it. She was serious enough about it that she'd created the "Dating Protocol," a set of rules that had to be followed if you wanted to be successful at "dating."

Not that the damn rules worked all the time.

Anyway, Spencer didn't want to be successful at dating. She wanted a real job at a real company. She wanted a career.

She was tired of "dating," sick of smiling at geriatric perverts with rheumy eyes and gnarled hands.

Despite the horrific interview, she was still determined to break the cycle of "dating" and had been thinking about how she might do that when Ben sat next to her on the park bench and said hello.

Not in the mood to talk to some strange guy, even if he was tall and good-looking, she'd mumbled a reply and contemplated moving to another bench.

"You okay?" he'd asked, his tone familiar, as if he knew her and was concerned.

"Not really," she'd admitted, finding herself unable to lie to him, somehow wanting to believe maybe he did care and wasn't just trying to hit on her.

"I didn't think so," he told her.

Sighing, she looked away for a moment and then back at him.

"You've been crying." It was a statement, not a question, more like an observation as he stared at her.

"So what if I have?" Spencer challenged, wishing there was more venom in her tone. "What the hell would you care?"

Had she asked him to care? Did she need him to care about her? Who was she to him except some girl he didn't know, sitting on a bench, near tears, wallowing in self-pity? She was just a dumb girl trying to figure out her life, which was steadily spinning out of control.

"I might care more than you think," he'd told her. "If you allow me to."

His response was annoying, and yet alluring, and Spencer found herself interested. Maybe not necessarily in him or his fake sympathy, but definitely in those diamond cuff links and the Rolex.

Her sister could get a lot of money for those items. Maybe even enough to cover this month's rent.

The way their arrangement worked, whatever Spencer stole, she gave to Rae, who fenced the stolen goods and then gave Spencer a cut.

But given her luck, her sister wouldn't get a tenth of what they were worth.

Despite her natural instinct to protect herself and her feelings, Spencer was intrigued by him, and a little entranced by his Island lilt, so she didn't turn him down when he asked her out to dinner.

She figured a good-looking Jamaican in a three-thousand-dollar suit was a decent prospect for fleecing. Even though she didn't want to "date" anymore, she had to, because the rent was due.

Although, if she "dated" him, she couldn't tell Rae.

The Dating Protocol rule stated that you could only "date" senior citizens, men over the age of sixty.

But Rae was always bending and breaking the rules, so what the hell?

Spencer's "date" that night with Ben Chang had been conflicting, a bit disturbing because Ben wasn't a typical "date."

Normally, she was never able to enjoy dinner and would push her food around the plate and sip seltzer water, which did little to calm her nervous stomach.

With Ben, she'd enjoyed the duck confit, microgreens, and sweetbreads and had eaten with relish, even allowing herself to indulge in a decadent chocolate mousse for dessert.

Their conversation had been easy and engaging. Talking to Ben was like talking to an old friend. He listened to her, and really seemed interested in what she cared about.

During a normal "date," the food and wine and boring conversation were something she had to suffer through, and while the "date" was enjoying her company, and probably thinking how he might coax her into bed later, Spencer was busy trying to remember if she'd brought everything she needed to "accomplish the goal," as Rae would say.

Oversized purse, to put the stolen goods in.

Latex gloves, so she wouldn't leave fingerprints.

Bear spray, in case the "date" got too aggressive before she could subdue him.

And most important of all, the small bottle of GHB, the elixir of oblivion, guaranteed to keep the target unconscious until the next day.

But she didn't "date" Ben that night, or the next time they went to dinner, or during their many impromptu picnics in Hermann Park, or when he surprised her with a weekend trip to the Cayman Islands. She kept reminding herself that she was supposed to "date" him, but she couldn't bring herself to go through with it.

And now two months later, she and Ben were in a strange, reluctant situation—not exactly a friendship, not quite a romantic relationship.

He was like a friend, but more than that; and yet, they weren't together.

Ben had respected their undefined relationship and still hadn't tried to seduce her, although she wouldn't have been adverse to a bit of coaxing, gentle or otherwise, especially when he kissed her goodnight.

Lots of goodnight kisses later, and now she was in bed with Ben Chang.

And maybe a bit in love with him, too.

Only a little bit, though, not too much in love.

But enough to make her realize that she had to put a stop to these feelings.

She couldn't risk falling more in love with Ben; she wasn't going to end up like her mother.

This past week, she'd realized that she had to end things with Ben. What she hadn't known was how she would leave him, or if she even could.

Most girls would be able to just walk away from him, and ignore his calls and texts, but she had a feeling he would be able to break down any resistance she managed to put up, and before she knew it, she'd be back in his bed, and he would be in her heart.

Spencer exhaled.

There was only one way to get herself out of this situation, only one way to make sure that love didn't leave her broken and damaged like her mother.

She would have to go through with her plans to "date" Ben.

Staring at the tray ceiling, Spencer focused on the mural above the bed. No, not a mural, she reminded herself. What had Ben called it? A silkscreen printing. Four panels, each one telling a story, which was something about a dragon and a tiger.

Bright, vivid, and lurid, it was a bloody, gory depiction of friendship, betrayal, deception, and death.

The first panel showed a large male tiger, a small tiger cub, and a baby dragon.

The tiger and the dragon grew up together, and they were as close as brothers despite their differences.

The second panel showed how the tiger and the dragon were trained to battle their enemies, depicted as various animals—rats, snakes, and oddly, even pigs and roosters.

In the third panel, the tiger and the dragon were fully grown. There was more fighting, bloody depictions of the tiger disemboweling pigs and roosters with his claws while the dragon used his fiery breath to burn his foes alive.

The fourth panel was strange; the tiger was shown allowing a man to put a yoke around his neck and lead him away, leaving the dragon to contend with a swarm of animals.

Fighting alone as the tiger grew smaller and smaller, the dragon prevailed, but at a price, as the very bottom of the panel showed him bloodied and battle-scarred.

Ben had said the last panel was about betrayal.

Spencer had wanted to know more, but didn't ask questions. Besides, it wasn't in the "Dating Protocol" to get to know more about the target, or—

Or … what the hell was she doing?

Staring at some gory mural, contemplating what it might mean.

She didn't have time for that.

Spencer sighed, her thoughts shifting to the strange nightmare again.

There was no reason to be spooked by it.

She'd heard someone explain that dreams were just the brain's way of ridding the subconscious of unnecessary images from various situations. Her nightmare had probably been a fusion of some soap opera she'd watched and a trashy book she'd read, nothing to overanalyze, or examine too closely.

The nightmare was nothing to worry about.

Or, was it?

What if the dream was trying to warn her?

What if her subconscious was telling her that "dating" Ben was a mistake, that she would get caught?

Although, if she got caught, Spencer knew it would be her own damn fault, because she hadn't followed the "Dating Protocol."

She was supposed to have made Ben a drink and put a few drops of GHB in it, which would have put him out for the rest of the night.

Spencer rolled over, wondering what the hell she was going to do.

Should she cut her losses and walk away with nothing to show for her trouble? Would that be the smart thing? Should she accomplish the "dating" goal? Or, forget about "dating" Ben and maybe find out if their random meeting in front of the reflecting pool at City Hall could develop into something more, something like …

Something like … what?

Love, marriage, baby carriage.

Spencer bristled. No, that would never happen. Love might blossom, she supposed. Anything was possible when emotions went awry. But kids? And marriage?

Marriage was a risk she wouldn't take.

Thanks to her mother, she knew that wedded bliss could blow up in your face.

After the honeymoon ended, her mother had morphed into something Spencer thought of as "that wife"—a clinging, desperate married woman obsessed with pleasing her husband, degrading and marginalizing herself, feverishly hoping that the wedding band would remain secure on her left finger.

Spencer had decided long ago that she would never willingly walk down the aisle and into a life of quiet desperation and indentured servitude, struggling in vain to be some kind of perfect wife for a man who didn't deserve her efforts, or affection.

Spencer sat up.

Enough with the damn thoughts about marriage and about a relationship with Ben because it wasn't going to happen.

Right now, he was her "date," not some romantic conquest, and she wasn't about to do something stupid like fall completely in love with him.

But she was going to rob him deaf, dumb, and blind.

2

Houston, Texas
Townhouse near Downtown

Wearing the short, tight bandage dress Ben Chang had practically ripped off hours ago, Spencer stood in the entryway of his walk-in closet.

She twisted the dimmer switch until a soft amber glow spread into the closet, just enough light to allow her to see.

Her pulse racing, she glanced around the large square space. Several wardrobes and ceiling-to-floor shelves ran along the perimeter, and in the middle was a closet island with more shelves and cabinets, all of it done in a black walnut finish with brushed nickel knobs and handles.

She took a few tentative steps on the dark hardwood floors, holding tight to the oversized Coach bag.

As she walked toward the island, it occurred to her that, technically, she'd breached the "Dating Protocol" again.

According to Rae's instructions, the bedroom should be checked first. Dresser and bureau drawers, bed tables, and even beneath mattresses. Once all valuables were removed, then you could check the closet.

Well, she hadn't been able to do that because Ben was *sleeping* in the large king-sized bed they'd made love in. He wasn't knocked out, slumped over unconscious on the couch, as he should have been, as he would have been if she had followed "Dating Protocol."

Spencer took a deep breath and tried to calm down.

Thankfully, she didn't feel sick like she had after her first "date."

Waves of nausea, spurred on by self-condemnation and shock at what she was about to do, had attacked her as she'd removed a Cartier watch from the dresser drawer of her "date," a crusty old professor with ashy skin.

When she'd told Rae, her sister rolled her eyes and made some dismissive comment about Spencer being melodramatic. But it hadn't been melodrama. It had been guilt, shame and the sick realization that she'd gotten to the point where she would actually steal.

Spencer took a step toward a rack of custom-made dress shirts, lined in a row, in various colors. Grabbing the sleeve of a pale blue shirt, she allowed the smooth fabric to slip between her fingers.

Honestly, she never would have started "dating" if she hadn't lost her job.

At first, she'd tried to be positive about the layoff and not think of it as the worst thing in the world; she tried to view it as an opportunity to get a better job, one she might enjoy, where she felt productive and appreciated by her bosses.

Six months later, she was still unemployed, but she hadn't been too worried that she hadn't yet found a job.

After all, she had unemployment checks. They wouldn't last forever, she knew, but she figured the money would last until she found a new job.

Three months after that, the unemployment benefits ran out, and she still wasn't gainfully employed.

Nine months after being let go, she found herself having to borrow rent money from her cousin Rusty Cane, a corporate attorney who made close to six figures, and having to pay her car note with money from her grandmother.

She had no viable source of income, no practical plan of action, and no idea how the hell she was going to survive.

All she had was a sly, savvy, older half-sister who made ends meet by "dating," something her sister confessed she'd been doing for the past year and a half, taking cash and watches and other expensive items from stupid old men.

Initially, Spencer wanted no part of "dating."

Prolonged unemployment was no excuse for engaging in a life of crime.

Many people who'd been laid off still had problems finding good jobs, and they didn't start lying, cheating, and drugging men, the hallmarks of Rae's "dating" scheme.

But Rae had given Spencer the hard sell, telling Spencer that the father they shared hadn't given them much. But he had given them very good genes.

"You're young and gorgeous, but that ain't gonna get you a job at a Fortune 500 company," Rae had told her. "Being beautiful will, however, get you a "date" with the CFO, and that dirty bastard, he won't give you a job, but he'll get off on the idea of screwing some girl young enough to be his daughter."

Spencer still hadn't been sure.

But when she'd asked for advice from her younger half-sister, Dennis-Andrea "Shady" Tanaka, she'd received a stern, rebuking lecture and an ominous warning.

"You're going to get caught, or worse," Shady said, sounding eerily prophetic. "Don't let Rae make you think that "dating" is your only option. You are a smart girl. You will get another job. You just have to believe and have faith …"

That had been easy for Shady to say since she had a damn job.

Turning from the shirts, Spencer walked around the island and stopped in front of two rows of drawers.

As much as she might want to, Spencer couldn't blame the choices she'd made on Rae. Her older half-sister hadn't twisted her arm or put a knife to her throat.

But Rae did have a very convincing argument.

"Girl, you can't keep wasting your time filling out online applications for jobs you're probably not gonna get," Rae had said. "And if you sign up with some temp agency, the most they're gonna offer you is twelve, maybe fifteen, an hour, and that ain't enough to pay your rent and your utilities and your car insurance and your student loans."

Her half-sister had been overbearing and persuasive, and while Spencer hadn't been exactly powerless to resist, she nevertheless hadn't put up much of a fight, even though she should have.

Resolving to get on with "accomplishing the goal," Spencer pulled out the top left drawer and found only underwear. The middle and bottom left drawers housed socks and white T-shirts. Worried, she pulled out the top right drawer. More underwear. She closed the top drawer and then pulled out the second drawer, hoping she wouldn't find more socks, or—

Spencer took a breath, staring into the drawer.

Guns. Three of them. Huge, black, and powerful.

She'd never come across any weapons before. Should she take them? Could Rae get any money for them?

She didn't know but wouldn't doubt it.

Rae was very resourceful and could unload just about anything. She seemed to have a potential buyer for everything.

But would Rae be okay with trying to sell three stolen guns?

Wary of the firearms, still unsure whether to take them or not, Spencer pulled the drawer out a bit further. In the back corner was a knife, the blade about three inches, the hilt made of jade, carved like a dragon.

She picked up the knife, examining the hilt. The dragon's eyes looked like real diamonds, but she wasn't sure. The body was expertly carved with scales and a long tail curving upward ending in a razor-sharp tip.

The knife was similar to the one she'd seen earlier in Ben's living room.

Spencer had never been to his townhouse before, and as he showed her around, she couldn't help but note the strong Asian influences in the décor, like some fusion of Feng Shui and Tang Dynasty.

The furnishings were dark, and most of the accent pieces had some type of dragon motif, from the cushions on the couch to the large Oriental rug beneath the long, family-style dining table.

Near an end table next to the couch, she'd spotted a large knife lying between a clock and small bonsai tree. The blade seemed longer than the heel on her stiletto, at least six inches, and the handle was a jade carving of two dueling dragons.

"Love and peace," he'd said, and she realized he'd seen her staring at it.

She looked up at him. "What do you mean?"

"One dragon lusts for love." He took a step toward her, close enough to put his arms around her, and she wanted him to, but he didn't. He stared at her with those darker than midnight eyes. "The other longs for peace. The blade is a symbol of death. In order for one to prevail, the other must perish."

"Is that so?" She tried to be sarcastic, trying to counter the effects of his gaze, to remember the goal she had to accomplish.

"The dragons are prepared to fight to the death," he told her, a hint of amusement in his dark gaze, making her wonder if he was serious or just trying to charm her. "But, they are immortal, and so their struggle will never end."

She hadn't commented at the time, unwilling to risk

becoming fascinated with him and his strange, mysterious conversation. But now that she had a few moments to reflect on his words, she recognized her own inner conflict. Her battle was between stealing and starving, doing what she knew was wrong while ignoring what she knew was right.

The "dating" would end for her eventually, sooner rather than later, she hoped.

But the memories would linger, and Spencer knew she would always struggle to reconcile the person she really was with the person she had allowed herself to become.

Despite her reservations, Spencer asked about the knife, and he'd told her it had been a gift, given to him by the man who'd raised him, the only father he'd ever known.

A bit confused, she asked, "You didn't grow up with your real father?"

"He was killed when I was a little boy."

"I'm sorry," she told him, and not just because of his loss, but because she never should have asked the question.

It was against "Dating Protocol" to question the "date" about anything personal.

"Don't be," he said, again with that spark of charm in his dark eyes. "No condolences for the weak."

Spencer had been surprised, and confused, by his response.

Her own father would never win any awards for loving and supportive parenting, but she would have been devastated if anything bad ever happened to him, even though he wouldn't deserve her tears.

Thinking Rae might be able to sell the knife, Spencer tossed it into the Coach bag.

Exhaling, she pulled out the bottom right drawer.

Holding in a squeal, she smiled a little, staring at two Rolexes and four stacks of one-hundred-dollar bills, each about one inch thick, rubber banded together.

The watches she expected; expensive timepieces were what

she usually came away with, along with jewelry. But she'd never found a drawer full of money before, and the sight of all those one-hundred-dollar bills took her breath away and had her trembling and a bit aroused, thinking of what she could do with all that cash.

There had to be about fifty thousand dollars, maybe more. Enough to pay all her bills for the next twelve months … well, maybe not for a whole year since she had to give Rae a cut.

A traitorous idea sprang forth in her mind, one she didn't push away.

What if she didn't tell Rae about the cash? Or, what if she told her half-sister she'd only found two stacks? Or maybe just one fat stack of cold, hard cash?

Spencer grabbed the stacks of money, shoved them into the Coach bag, and then reached for the watches.

Once everything was in the purse, she rose to her feet.

Turning, she headed out of the closet, her stomach churning.

With each step she took, her panic and hesitation grew.

The Coach bag was heavy, as though filled with the weight of her sins …

Sins she didn't have to commit.

Ben didn't know she'd just been in his closet stealing from him. There was still time to turn around and put the money and the watches back in the drawer where she'd found them.

But if she did that, it would mean she wouldn't be "dating" Ben.

And if she wasn't going to "date" him, then what was she going to do?

Get to know him better? Try to see if they could have a real relationship?

Fall a little bit more in love with him?

No, no, no, that couldn't happen. She wouldn't let that happen.

She didn't want to fall deeper in love. She knew how that

ridiculous tale of woe ended. She wasn't going to end up desperate and depressed when he woke up one morning and decided she wasn't good enough.

After witnessing all of her mother's trials and tribulations with men, Spencer had promised herself she would never lose her mind over a man, and she'd meant it. She wasn't going to break that promise—no matter how she felt about Ben Chang.

3

Houston, Texas
Townhouse near Downtown

As Spencer turned the dimmer switch and darkness blanketed the closet again, she was sick with regret and guilt, second-guessing herself, wondering if she was doing the right thing, no longer sure that "dating" Ben Chang was what she really wanted to do.

And what would Ben think when he realized his money and watches were gone? Would he suspect her? Would he call the cops on her? Or maybe come after her himself?

Spencer took a deep breath and told herself to get a handle on her wayward emotions.

She had to be practical, rational.

The truth was, she would never see Ben again anyway.

According to Rae's "Dating Protocol," you could only "date" a man once.

After "dating" him, you were forbidden to see him again because there was a chance, though slim, that he might remember you. The GHB was supposed to be a mind-altering memory eraser, but it was possible that you might not have given the date enough of the drug, and the next day, his mind could be flooded with strange memories. He might experience fuzzy recollections of you handing him a cognac before his world went dark, and he could start to get suspicious.

Especially when he discovered his ten-thousand-dollar diamond cufflinks were missing.

Spencer took a deep breath and thought about the GHB.

She hadn't used it on Ben because before she could suggest a glass of wine, he'd pulled her into his arms for a kiss.

And that kiss had led to more kisses.

Soon, she forgot about "dating," and stealing from him as the swirling between her legs became insistent. All she wanted was to feel him inside her.

Spencer cursed.

The GHB protocol breach was dangerous. It was stupid to steal from a man who wasn't drugged out of his mind, but it was too late to turn back. There was nothing she could do about it now.

Except leave.

She needed to leave right now, while Ben was still sleeping, before she lost her nerve. She could slip out of the townhouse and wouldn't have to worry about facing him in the morning, when he would wake up alone, without her.

And he might wonder where she was, and maybe look for her, and not finding her in the shower, or in the kitchen, or anywhere in the townhouse, he might become worried.

He might call her, but she wouldn't answer the phone.

He would probably leave messages, asking why she'd left without saying goodbye. And she wouldn't be able to tell him the truth, that she cared about him, but there were some risks she couldn't take, not even for a life of luxury and comfort.

Heavy-hearted, Spencer tiptoed back into the bedroom. An

amber glow from an outside street lamp seeped into the darkness, providing a hint of light, enough to see the king-sized bed was empty.

Confused, her pulse racing, she stared at the rumpled sheets, which looked as though they had been pushed back.

Trembling, Spencer took a step toward the bed.

Where was Ben? Why wasn't he still in bed? Why would he have gotten up? Where would he go at three o'clock in the morning? What could have awakened him?

Cotton-mouthed, Spencer sank down on the bed. Had she woken up Ben when she'd eased out of bed?

Against her will, unfounded conclusions rushed into her mind, convincing her that Ben hadn't been sleeping when she'd tiptoed into his closet.

He must have been watching her as she put her dress back on, and he might have been confused, thinking she was leaving.

Until he saw her head into the closet with her purse.

Spencer pressed her lips together, trying to stop the scream rising in her throat. How could she have been so stupid! Why hadn't she drugged Ben? Why hadn't she followed the damn protocol?

She knew the damn rules. Drug your "date," and then wait until he was knocked out cold before you go rummaging through his stuff. How many damn times had Rae told her that? Why the hell had she thought Ben would just lie there and sleep, giving her all the time she needed to rob him? She should have known better. She did know better. That's why she wanted to kick herself for making this stupid mistake.

She took a deep breath and tried to stay calm, but it was impossible.

All she could think was the worst.

Ben must have found out she'd stolen from him, and soon, she would hear sirens and see red and blue flashing lights. Ben would get the police to come in and arrest her, and then what the hell would she do?

She had no idea, but she wasn't sticking around to find out.

Clutching the Coach bag, Spencer jumped up from the bed and hurried toward the bedroom's double doors. Yanking one door open, she dashed out into the hall and headed down the stairs to the second floor. In the large living room, she ran past two black leather chairs and a large black leather couch, the pieces separated by a low, square coffee table.

She had to get out of the townhouse before Ben caught her, and she prayed she would, even though she had no right to ask for divine protection.

Stealing was a sin, and if Ben caught her and beat the hell out of her, then maybe she would deserve it.

Trying to keep her mounting panic at bay, Spencer hurried toward the wide, arched entryway leading out to the second-floor landing. Passing under the archway, she glanced right, over the balustrade with its ornate, black wrought-iron spindles.

Ben was heading up the staircase.

Dressed in boxing pants and nothing else, he looked huge and fierce as he took the stairs two at a time until he reached the landing.

Panic gripped her, and she froze, not sure what to do, barely able to think over the roaring in her head.

Stalking toward her and scowling, Ben raised his arm.

In his right hand was a large, black pistol, the barrel pointing at her face.

Raw, searing terror expanded within her, pushing away all doubt and confusion.

Ben was going to kill her.

And she knew it was because she was a thief and a liar, who deserved to be shot full of holes.

"Ben, please!" she cried out, stumbling backwards. "Don't—"

The gun went off, the sound subtle, almost like the pistol was muffled, but it sent her heart into her throat, nearly choking her as she lunged away from Ben toward one of the chairs.

Spencer stumbled, screaming as she skidded across the hardwood floor. Slipping, she hit the floor and rolled over onto her back. Moving over onto her hip, dazed and disoriented, she pushed herself up to a sitting position and then scrambled to crawl away from Ben.

Clutching the Coach purse, she moved her arms and knees as quick as she could, confused, desperate to escape before Ben killed her.

Surveying her surroundings, Spencer felt her stomach drop and fought the urge to beat her fists against the hardwood floor, realizing she'd crawled the wrong way.

She was behind the damn couch!

Heart slamming, Spencer flattened herself on the hardwood floor, trying not to move.

She had to figure out how to get the hell away from Ben before he put a bullet between her eyes.

"Spencer ..."

She squeezed her eyes shut, staying quiet, trying to come up with a plan of escape, and if escape was not possible, then she needed a plan of defense. But how the hell could she defend herself? Ben had a damn gun, and what the hell did she have?

The bear spray?

Maybe.

But could she get it out of the purse without Ben noticing? She didn't think so. Ben wouldn't give her a chance to reach into the Coach bag. If he caught her before she could escape the townhouse, he would force her to keep her hands where he could see them, and—

"Sweet girl."

Ice shot through her veins, and she went numb, her mind

contaminated by thoughts of Ben shooting her and then dumping her bullet-riddled body into the muddy waters of Buffalo Bayou.

"Don't hide from me."

His Island lilt was soft, and yet sinister, shaking her, rocking her just as fiercely as the many orgasms he'd given her when they'd made love.

"Spencer."

Somehow, thinking about the sex they'd had gave her a strange, desperate hope. He'd made love to her as if his life depended on it, and at times, his caress seemed almost savage. But he'd been just as tender, giving her sweet, slow kisses in the most intimate places.

Maybe, just maybe, there was still part of him that cared for her. Maybe she could appeal to the tenderness and coax him into being the man who'd sat next to her on the park bench.

She didn't know, but she had to try.

She couldn't let him shoot her down like a dog in the street. She couldn't—

Ben's footsteps came closer to the back of the couch, slow and deliberate.

Slipping her arm through the handles of the purse, Spencer rose to her knees and crawled the length of the back of the couch, palms against the cool hardwood as she hurried to escape his approaching footsteps.

Hoping and praying he wouldn't catch her, she advanced toward the end table and then crawled around it, stopping when she saw the archway leading out to the landing and trying to calculate the distance—

"Spencer ..."

Fear washed over her.

Ben's voice was too close, and when she glanced up over her shoulder, her terror was confirmed. Her mind in turmoil, Spencer crawled forward, all thoughts of trying to rationalize with Ben fleeing, being replaced by thoughts of escape.

Ben stepped in front of her, blocking her.

Cautious and trembling, Spencer lifted her eyes to stare at him and then rose to her feet. "Don't hurt me, please …"

Frowning, Ben reached a hand toward her, but she stepped back, avoiding his grasp.

"Stay away from me!" she warned, and as she moved backward toward the chairs, she opened the purse and reached inside, feeling for the bear spray. "Please just let me go!"

Something sharp sliced her finger.

The knife!

She'd forgotten about the dragon-hilt knife she'd put in her purse.

"You're not going anywhere," he said, stepping toward her and grabbing her arm.

"Let me go!" She wrapped her hand around the hilt of the knife, pulled it from the Coach purse, and plunged the knife toward him.

The blade sank into his abdomen, to the left of his navel.

He released her, cursing and trying to pull the knife from his gut.

Frantic, Spencer turned and sprinted toward the archway. From the landing, she headed down the stairs, not bothering to look back as she descended the staircase and stumbled down the steps.

In the foyer, she staggered to the front door.

With trembling fingers, she worked to unlock the deadbolt. Desperate to get out and fumbling with the lock, Spencer glanced behind her, looking up the stairs. Ben stood on the second floor landing, staggering as he stared down at her, the hilt of the dragon knife still protruding from his gut.

Seconds later, he dropped to his knees and tumbled down the steps.

Spencer screamed.

Landing on the floor in the foyer, Ben rolled onto his back and stared up at her.

"Sweet girl ..." he rasped. "Help me ..."

Spencer turned from him, yanking the doorknob and twisting it.

Crying and ignoring Ben's pleas for help, she pulled the door open and ran out of the house in a blind, terrified panic.

4

San Ignacio, Belize
Belizean Banyan Resort – Owner's Office

Sione Tuiali'i sat in his office, staring toward the sliding glass doors, which opened to the private terrace. Beyond the limestone rectangle, an expansive stretch of lawn sloped down toward the jungle that surrounded the thirty-six-casita resort he owned and managed.

Absently, his eyes wandered back to his desk to a proposal to host a retreat for a group of wedding planners written on the resort's letterhead.

As he read the proposal again, for the fourth, or maybe fifth time, he felt something wasn't right, but he couldn't put his finger on the problem, whether it was grammatical or contextual, which bothered him.

He'd never had a problem writing business proposals before, but today he felt ...

Sione wasn't sure how he felt. He couldn't really define the emotions.

But he knew why the uneasiness vexed him, conjuring up

memories he always fought so hard to forget, remnants of the past he struggled to put behind him.

A past that always threatened to resurrect itself.

No matter how deep Sione tried to bury it, he feared he could never dig a grave deep enough that the past couldn't claw its way out of somehow.

Standing, he pushed a hand into the pocket of his slacks and fingered the small piece of metal lodged there, the connection to memories he didn't want to revisit.

Reluctant, he withdrew his hand, opened it, and stared at the pendant in his palm.

It was a small silver tiger, the last tangible link to his former life, to the person he'd once been, the person he hoped he would never be again ...

Once it had hung from a thin chain, but the eighteen inches of white gold had been taken from him, snatched from his neck one balmy night, the air heavy with the scent of damp earth, pungent vegetation, and impending rain.

He'd accidentally found the metal tiger this morning while hunting for his watch.

The old Timex wasn't worth much, but Siosi Tuiali'i had always worn it, and after inheriting the watch, Sione had made a point to wear it every day, in memory of his uncle.

He'd been frustrated by the misplaced timepiece and had resorted to searching the most unlikely places, one of which was his bottom bureau drawer.

His uncle's watch wasn't the only thing he'd found.

In the far right corner, behind an old T-shirt, was the silver tiger.

Small and gleaming, about the size of a .22 caliber bullet.

The tiger crouched, his prey in sight, ready to pounce.

Sione wasn't superstitious, but he couldn't help think the tiger was a bad omen.

He'd been wary of touching it.

Ten years had passed since he'd worn it, or even thought about it, and for some reason, he thought touching it would be like sliding his fingers across a talisman, but instead of good luck, the tiger pendant would bring potent destruction and bad tidings.

Still, he'd put it in his pocket and brought it to the office.

After his day was officially over, before he went back to the owner's casita, he planned to take a detour through the jungle and drop the pendant in a thick tangle of brush, where it would be lost forever ...

And maybe, the memories of his former life would disappear as well.

But he wasn't getting his hopes up.

The past would show up again, like it had today.

And like it had three months ago, when he'd answered his cell without checking the Caller ID and realized too late that he'd answered a call from the one person he never wanted to have anything to do with.

Richard Tuiali'i.

His father.

The call hadn't come out of the blue, though.

Every six months or so, his father would reach out, and Sione would shrink back, usually ignoring his father's attempts at reconciliation.

The call three months ago had been different.

Different enough for Sione to take notice and to wonder if maybe it was time to investigate the possibility of ending their ten-year estrangement.

Maybe.

But after a few weeks of awkward, tentative conversations, Sione's wariness returned.

Talking to his father was risky.

Richard had always been one to take a mile when given an inch.

It wasn't long before Sione went back to not accepting his father's calls, and eventually Richard got the hint.

But just because Richard had stopped calling didn't mean he'd given up.

Sione knew better than that.

His father was tenacious and relentless, and when he wanted something, he did whatever it took to get it, no matter the cost.

Sione's desk phone rang, and he pushed the 'Speaker' button and then answered.

It was his cousin Truman Camareno, who was also his lawyer and business advisor.

"You're going out with me and Micah tonight, right?" Truman asked.

"When did you get here?" Sione asked.

"Flew in yesterday," Truman said. "And I'm only staying a week, just to help you out with the negotiations."

"Well ..." Sione hedged, thinking about the negotiations.

For some time, Sione had been mulling over the idea of building a few "guest tree houses" to expand the lodging opportunities at the Belizean Banyan, and hopefully attract a different market of travelers, those who might be looking for a more adventurous jungle experience.

For the past six months, he'd been searching for the perfect section of land to build on and had found several acres of rainforest that backed up against the property line of the resort.

His agent had contacted the seller and expressed serious interest in buying, and initially, the family who owned the land had expressed serious interest in selling.

But recent family squabbles had stalled the deal, and Sione was pissed that it might fall through because one of the sisters was apprehensive and questioning whether or not their deceased father really would have wanted the land sold.

Probably, the sister just wanted more money, or a bigger slice of the pie.

Nevertheless, Sione was prepared to make concessions, or even increase his offer, which Truman would most likely advise against, but Sione didn't care how much money he had to shell out, or what he had to mortgage or leverage.

The land deal had to go through.

The "guest tree houses" had been his idea and would be his first contribution to the expansion of the resort, without his uncle's guidance, and he was prepared to do whatever it took to make it happen.

Because failure wasn't an option.

Failure would give those who doubted him a legitimate right to claim that the resort would fall apart under his direction and management.

Acquiring the land for the "guest tree houses" was Sione's first test, and if he didn't pass it, then his failure might be seen as proof that he didn't have what it took to be a hotel owner.

After all, it wasn't a property he'd built. It was a successful, thriving resort that had been given to him by his uncle Siosi Tuiali'i, a compassionate and pious man who'd rescued Sione from a path of self-destruction almost a decade earlier.

Three years ago when his uncle passed away, Sione had inherited Belizean Banyan Resort, a five-star property in the heart of the Belizean jungle.

Now, Sione had to prove that his uncle hadn't made a mistake when he'd willed the resort to him. He had to let everyone know he was a capable businessman and could handle the demanding and sometimes difficult job.

More than anything, he was determined to show the naysayers that he deserved the good fortune his uncle had bequeathed to him.

Because most days, he didn't think he did.

"Speaking of the negotiations," Sione started. "I was thinking—"

"Listen, we'll negotiate tomorrow," Truman promised. "I'll get you that land, and you won't have to pay an arm and a leg for it, trust me, okay? Tonight, let's go out, have a good time."

Sione sighed.

He didn't really want to go out with his cousins; he tended to make bad decisions when he went out, and drank too damn much, but—

"So, we'll see you around ten?" Truman asked, but it was more like a command than a question.

"Yeah," Sione capitulated. "See you then."

5

San Ignacio, Belize
Belizean Banyan Resort — Owner's Casita

Sione stood in the middle of his bedroom, shaking his head as he looked around, memories of last night flooding him with regret and disappointment.

Bright, unrelenting sunlight slashed through the glass pocket doors that opened to the terrace, exposing remnants of wanton debauchery.

A few shot glasses, his shirt, an empty bottle of tequila, several discarded condoms, a woman's strappy heel, a short, practically see-thru dress, his pants, and a wine glass stained with red lipstick.

The harsh morning glare exposed everything, and with no fuzzy, clouded recollections to hide behind, he was forced to take a long, unflinching look at his mistakes.

His gaze moved to the bed, where the naked woman lay, bed linens twisted in and around her arms and legs, providing peeks of her ass and breasts.

Last night's latest conquest.

No, conquest was the wrong word. She hadn't played hard to get, and really, he never had problems attracting women, never had to convince, or cajole, some girl into his bed. Women had always found him good-looking, and his height and muscular build had never hurt his chances.

Last night's mistake was more like it.

Another mistake he shouldn't have made.

Like the mistake he'd made two days ago

And the mistake one night last week, and the mistake from a week before that.

He had never been a fan of inconsequential sex, even though he indulged every now and then. But his infrequent, inconsequential hook-ups were becoming disturbingly more frequent and more consequential.

And less enjoyable.

There was always physical release, but that could be accomplished alone.

He felt like he was looking for something he would never find, something that didn't really exist, a connection with a soul mate.

With no one special in his life, and no current potential prospects, the occasional hook-ups were increasingly frustrating, reminding him that he'd blown his chance at love.

Or rather, what he'd mistakenly assumed was love.

Two years ago, his engagement to a beautiful, caring, intelligent woman had been shot to hell, for various reasons, most of which he didn't like to think about.

He was starting to wonder if the trivial sex was some kind of pathological response to the destruction of a relationship he'd hoped would last forever.

Although destruction probably wasn't the right word, wasn't strong enough.

Annihilation was probably better; the relationship had been utterly destroyed.

But if he was honest, the connection hadn't been as solid as he'd told himself it was, hadn't been as genuine as he'd wished it was.

The truth was, he hadn't really been in love.

When the relationship blew up in their faces, he might have been more relieved than disappointed, but the weapon used to blow them apart had left him bitter and vengeful.

Not in the mood for desolate reflections and introspection, his gaze moved to the woman lying naked in the bed. What was her name? Kimberley, Karen, Kayla?

He couldn't remember, and it didn't matter.

The hook-up was already over, less than twenty-four hours after it had begun the night before at some club his cousins Truman and Micah, had dragged him to.

Sione hadn't wanted to go, but his cousins thought he was working too hard, thought he was spending too much time trying to live up to a legacy, desperate to meet what his cousins felt were self-imposed expectations.

But they didn't understand.

They had worked for their success.

Truman had gotten a degree in finance and worked as a financial analyst before going back to school to become lawyer and was now a successful plaintiff's attorney. Micah had decided to become an accountant, and he was Truman's bookkeeper.

Sione's accomplishments weren't from his own sweat and tears.

Any success he enjoyed had been handed down to him from his uncle.

"Wake up, beautiful ..." Sione sat on the edge of the bed and touched her shoulder. "Time to get going."

Moaning, the woman rolled over on her back; her eyes fluttered open, and she gave him a slow, lazy smile. "What time is it?"

Time for you to get the hell out of my casita and out of my life, he thought.

But he smiled and said, "It's a little after nine …"

"Nine? I'm usually up at five!" Giggling, she rose up, arching her back so the bed sheets slid down and pooled around her waist, giving him a view of her breasts that didn't quite spur him into action. "I typically have an early work-out, then some breakfast, but since I'm on vacation, I guess I'm allowed to oversleep."

"Sorry you missed breakfast," he told her. "But we have three restaurants at the resort, if you're still hungry."

"I'm very hungry," she told him, moving onto his lap, then placing her hands on his shoulders as she angled her head to press her lips against his neck. "And I know exactly what I want."

Arms encircling her waist, he said, "Bacon and eggs."

She rose up and then straddled him, and as he stared at her breasts, he wasn't excited.

There was nothing special about this woman, nothing to differentiate her from any of his other bad decisions.

At nine in the morning, and slightly hungover, he found her remarkably unappealing, and the lusty gaze she gave him was more vapid porn queen than sexy vixen, which was what she was probably trying to be.

He hoped she didn't expect a few rounds of morning lovemaking, because he wasn't in the mood. He'd completely lost interest.

Not that he'd ever been interested in her, even after a few glasses of wine last night. She was just some woman he'd met in a bar. He hadn't really gotten to know anything about her, but as she'd stood too close to him, accidentally on purpose brushing her taut nipples against him as they made small talk, eventually he grew horny enough to indulge in what she'd been offering.

Several hours of unabashed, uninhibited sex had left him satisfied, but they hadn't connected, and he was pissed that he'd succumbed to another one-night stand.

"Listen, Kimberley," he began.

Giving him a tight smile, she said, "Kelsey …"

Oh, yeah, that's right, Kelsey. That was her name.

She smiled, then lifted her leg, snaked it around him, and then twined her other leg around his waist so that her legs were locked behind his back, and she started to move her hips.

"I'm in the mood for a long, thick juicy sausage …"

He wasn't surprised she'd said that, but he wasn't hungry for her; last night's taste was more than enough. He'd had seconds and thirds, and his appetite for her was gone.

Besides, he'd had enough of her wailing and screeching and her dirty talk, which had been more amusing than arousing.

"Kelsey …" He grabbed her hips and stopped her movement. "I would love to, but right now is not a good time …"

"I don't understand." She frowned and looked confused. "Why not?"

"Listen, believe me, I would absolutely love to stay in bed with you all day," he lied, giving her what he hoped was an apologetic smile. "But I have a meeting this morning that I can't be late for."

Her green eyes a bit suspicious, she said, "I thought you owned the place."

Nodding, he said, "Yeah, I do own the place."

"Well, then it's okay if you're late for the meeting," she said, wrapping her arms around him. "Since you know the owner."

"This meeting is with my brokers," he said, removing her arms. "I can't be late, and I need to meet with my assistant to get some documents together, so …"

"So …" She tried to smile, but he could tell she was a bit embarrassed as she moved away and pulled the bed linens around her body, trying to cover herself, avoiding his gaze. "I probably should get going, right?"

Feeling like an asshole, he said, "Look, it's not that I don't want you to stay, it's just that these meetings might be tense, and they'll probably last all day, and—"

"No, I understand," she said, sneaking a quick glance at him and then looking away again, becoming interested in the abstract patterns on the Egyptian cotton sheets. "I've got a full day, too."

"Sightseeing?"

"Mayan ruins," she said, her voice flat.

"Xunantunich?"

She nodded, tucking her long, wavy hair behind her ears.

"It's a good day to go," he said, feeling the need to extend the small talk, thinking that maybe his feigned interest in her sightseeing might take the sting out of his rejection. "The cruise ships won't be docking today, so it shouldn't be too crowded."

She nodded. "That's good to know."

"Yeah," he said and stood. "So ..."

"Um, listen I don't want to be a chore, but would it be okay if I take a shower?" she asked, glancing up at him, biting her bottom lip. "And then let myself out?"

He didn't really like the idea of leaving her alone in his casita, but he needed to get to his meeting, and he felt bad about kicking her out. He didn't want to be a complete asshole.

"Yeah," he told her. "That's fine."

6

Houston, Texas
Moonlight Lake Apartments

Spencer stared at the untouched mimosa in front of her on the small, metal table, afraid to look at her sisters.

It was ten in the morning, and she, Rae, and Shady were out on the small patio connected to Rae's one-bedroom apartment off South Main.

Already, the temperature was close to eighty degrees, promising another typical Houston day in May—hot, humid, and overcast with a few peeks of sun, glowing shafts of light shooting through swirling bluish-gray clouds.

Clustered around the table, Spencer and her sisters might have been gossiping about men and sex, looking more like a trio of sorority sisters than three twenty-something women who regularly complained about the same inattentive, neglectful father.

If not for the man who'd slept with, and then summarily discarded, all three of their mothers, Spencer doubted they would have been friends. They might have even been rivals, competing for the same men, each one impressed by and yet jealous of the other girl's beauty.

They probably would have been just like their mothers, cutthroat enemies who'd grown to hate each other after they'd each found out that the same man had made a fool of them.

Or maybe she and her sisters wouldn't have been enemies.

But Spencer knew they wouldn't have had anything to do with each other. They hardly had anything in common; and their differences went well beyond their looks, which were so contrasting that people often had a hard time believing they were related.

Shady, whose mother was Japanese, had honey-kissed skin and a long column of stick-straight, oil-black hair; Rae was a caramel-hued stunner with gray eyes and natural dark brown cork-screw curls with ginger and butterscotch highlights; and Spencer had the smooth milk chocolate complexion, perfect bone structure, and a magnetic sexiness that attracted men indiscriminately.

She and her sisters couldn't have been more *not* alike.

Shady was a sweet-natured, church-going optimist; Rae was tough and fearless with her brazen take-no-prisoners attitude; and Spencer was a study in contrasts, generous, but bitchy, loyal and selfish, bold and yet unsure of herself, often lamenting her decisions.

Sometimes, Spencer was amazed at how close they'd become since finding out they were related, almost seven years ago. It could have gone terribly. They could have fought like wildcats and disowned each other. But their bond had been instant and had remained indestructible.

Last night had been a testament to their connection.

After her horrific ordeal, her sisters had been her lifeline, and Spencer thanked God for them. She prayed they would understand her actions and they wouldn't condemn her for what she'd done.

"Honey, can you tell us what happened last night?" Shady prodded, her voice gentle, encouraging.

Sighing, Spencer stared at the condensation trailing down the side of the glass tumbler, like the sweat rolling down her back.

It was time for explanations, and maybe champagne and orange juice would give her the courage, but she doubted it.

Last night, she'd had an excuse to put off telling her sisters about her ordeal.

Still numb from fear and self-loathing, the events a confusing jumble in her mind, she knew she couldn't give them a cohesive linear account. At best, she might have been able to mumble a haphazard, disjointed retelling. She'd been too rattled and shell-shocked. Rae and Shady had agreed she needed to rest and they could talk in the morning.

Which had come too quickly.

But night hadn't passed fast enough, and it was hard to believe she'd made it through the midnight hours without going insane.

She'd been plagued by nightmares, gruesome kaleidoscopic images of being chased by some bloody creature she couldn't quite make out, but that she suspected was Ben Chang, or maybe even herself.

Several times during the night, she'd had to force herself awake to escape the terrorizing dreams.

And as she sat up, gasping and panting, the cotton bed sheet Rae had given her to ward off the chill of the A/C would be soaked and twisted around her body. Once, she'd awakened to find the sheet wound around her throat, as she imagined Ben's hands would be when he came after her.

When shafts of light blasting through the vertical mini-blinds in front of the sliding patio doors awakened her, she didn't remember where she was. She didn't know why she was sleeping on Rae's lumpy, threadbare couch, and not in her own bed.

Sitting up and wiping crust from her eyes, the memories came back like a flood washing over her and nearly drowning her.

She'd stabbed Ben ... left him bleeding on the floor, begging her for help, but she'd been too terrified to turn back and had run out of the townhouse and down the street ... through the maze of narrow roads marred by ridges of broken concrete and potholes. She ran like the devil was chasing her, not looking back, too afraid she would see Ben right on her heels, holding the bloody knife he'd pulled from his gut, eager to cut her heart out.

Dazed and disoriented, she'd made her way to a twenty-four-hour Walgreens, where she'd called Shady.

Half an hour later, both her sisters arrived to pick her up.

From their frowns and sly, worried glances, she knew they had questions and wanted answers, but they put off the interrogation and focused on getting her into the backseat of Rae's hand-me-down compact, where she curled into the fetal position and wept silently.

"Girl, what the hell happened to you last night?" Rae demanded, her voice like a gunshot, startling Spencer from her disturbing reverie.

Panic snaking through her, Spencer blurted out, "I stabbed Ben."

7

San Ignacio, Belize
Belizean Banyan Resort

After a quick glance at the old Timex his uncle used to wear, Sione headed along the familiar gravel and crushed shell path, which curved, twisted, and wound through the jungle before opening to wide swaths of manicured lawn that led down grassy slopes and up hills dotted with hibiscus bushes.

As he passed the walkways that led to the various guest casitas, he still couldn't believe the luxury resort in the Belizean jungle was really his.

No one had been more shocked than he had when his uncle's probate attorney informed him that his uncle had willed the resort to him.

He hadn't expected so much from the man who'd already given him more than he deserved.

Upon learning that he was the new owner of the Belizean resort, he'd felt both galvanized and paralyzed. He'd been eager to make sure the property stayed profitable and to build on the foundation of his uncle's success.

At the same time, he felt stuck, fearful of moving forward, worried that without his uncle's presence, he would flounder and become frustrated and retreat back to a life he was more familiar, and comfortable with, despite living ten years under his uncle's protective wing.

Three years later, he still sometimes felt as though he didn't deserve the resort, that his uncle made a mistake leaving it to him.

And he wasn't the only one who felt that way.

His uncle's children—Sione's cousins, five Wharton graduates who were based in Hawaii and oversaw the properties in the Pacific—were convinced he didn't deserve the opportunity to manage the Belizean Banyan.

They firmly believed that Sione had coerced their father into leaving him the resort, and they'd accused Sione of using threats and strong-arm tactics, throwing his past in his face.

Sione had come from a life of violence and intimidation, and his cousins were convinced he'd taken advantage of their father's generous and compassionate nature, which included rescuing a then sixteen-year-old Sione from a life of self-destruction and raising him like one of his own sons.

Well, no, that wasn't exactly true.

His cousins had set him straight.

Siosi Tuiali'i had never thought of him as a son, and as for snatching Sione out of the fire, well, that kind act had actually been motivated by Siosi's animosity toward his brother Richard, who was Sione's father.

Still, Sione believed his uncle had saved his life, and he'd been grateful for the gift, which he'd received with excitement and a little trepidation.

Sione had initially thought his cousins might contest the will, but they'd honored their father's wishes. After all, the Belizean resort paled in comparison to the Pacific real estate empire, which stretched from California to Japan. They weren't going to waste their time fighting him for one resort in Belize.

They would rather sit back, wait for him to fail miserably, and then take over.

Continuing down the path, Sione pushed his skeptical cousins from his mind.

The smell of bark, cinnamon, and hibiscus and the sun beating down on his back, penetrating the cotton-blend short-sleeved polo, heralded the start of another nice day, but he doubted he'd get to enjoy it.

He was still wary about the bad decision he'd left in his casita.

And he wasn't feeling very optimistic about the business meeting.

He hadn't lied to Kimberley ... or was it Kelsey ...?

Whatever her name was, he'd been telling the truth. He had to meet with his real estate brokers, and he wasn't looking forward to it. He had a feeling he was going to hear bad news about the property he hoped to purchase.

Sione stopped, realizing he'd forgotten some important documents.

Ahead, beyond a row of tall Queen Palms, he saw the rear of the administrative building and debated whether to go back for the reports or not.

The documents had been emailed to him a few days ago from his accountant. He could access the email from his office at the administrative building, but the copy sitting on his desk back at the casita had his hand-written notes, and he needed them for the meeting.

Cursing, Sione turned and headed back to the casita.

8

Houston, Texas
Moonlight Lake Apartments

"You stabbed Ben?" Rae jumped up, let loose a stream of curses, her customary vile, vulgar response and then sat back down, frowning, her nostrils flaring.

"Oh my God, Spencer, why?" Shady asked. "What happened?"

"I didn't have a choice," Spencer rushed to say, hoping to circumvent any judgment or suspicion. "I had to."

Rae cursed again. "What does that mean, you had to?"

"Ben tried to kill me."

Shady's dark eyes clouded with apprehension. "He tried to kill you?"

"What the—" Rae stopped, shaking her head, and then said, "Start from the damn beginning. Don't leave anything out."

Spencer sighed and hesitated, not sure how much of the story she would tell them.

Or how much she could tell them.

Or how much she *should* tell them, rather.

Last night, tossing and turning on Rae's lumpy couch, when

she wasn't reliving the moment when she had sunk that blade into Ben's gut, she was going over the details of her last encounter with Ben from the dinner date, to the lovemaking, to the money and watches she'd stolen, and finally back to the moment when she'd had no choice but to stab him.

It wasn't because she was trying to kill him, but because it had been her only means of defense.

Ben had pointed a gun in her face and he'd shot at her. Her only thought had been survival, doing whatever she had to so he wouldn't blow her head off.

As for what to tell Rae and Shady, Spencer figured she would leave out the lovemaking.

Her sisters didn't need to know she'd slept with Ben, especially since she'd spent the last two months claiming they weren't engaged in an intimate relationship.

She usually told Rae and Shady everything, but one subject remained off-limits: her love life.

Which she'd always said was non-existent, the way she preferred it.

Not to say that she didn't go out from time to time, because she did, but she knew that if she mentioned a guy to her sisters, they would jump to conclusions and have her married and pregnant in a matter of minutes.

And she especially didn't want to hear anything about getting married.

Marriage was too risky. She couldn't take the chance of turning into "that wife."

Her sisters thought her crazy "that wife" theories were just an excuse. Rae thought she didn't want to get married because she didn't want to have sex with the same man for the rest of her life. Shady believed that their father's rampant, unabashed unfaithfulness made Spencer reluctant to commit.

The truth was a lot simpler, a bit more complex, and had everything to do with Spencer's mother.

"Girl, are you deaf?" Rae asked.

"Spencer, we just want to help," Shady said. "Tell us what happened."

Picking up the damp glass tumbler, Spencer took a sip of the mimosa, hoping the champagne and orange juice would help her figure out what to say, because she still wasn't really sure.

As for her decision to "date" Ben, Spencer would admit that and try to explain her reasoning.

She would cop to stealing the watches, but she wasn't going to tell them about the cash.

It wasn't because she didn't want to share the loot.

For some reason, she had a feeling the money shouldn't be spent.

No, it was more like the money *couldn't* be spent because if it was, something bad might happen.

Putting the glass back on the table, knowing she could no longer hesitate, Spencer said, "Last night, Ben and I went out to dinner ..."

"Is that the beginning?" Rae demanded, her gray eyes narrowed.

Spencer wasn't sure where the beginning was or what it should be. The question of where to start was almost impossible because it wasn't clear.

Each moment has its own beginning, its own anniversary, and even its own ending.

Sometimes, the beginning was significant, and other times it didn't matter.

But the truth was, the beginning was when she'd met Ben Chang.

The day he'd sat next to her on that park bench had started a chain reaction of events that led to feelings she didn't think she would be able to control, feelings that would lead to emotional demise if she allowed them to have their way.

Their two-month friendship had always been on the verge of

exploding, or maybe imploding, into something more, something she'd always told herself she didn't want.

She'd started to fall in love with Ben and she'd panicked.

Those feelings were like a fire, a spark that turned into a flame that quickly spread, raging and burning, threatening to grow into an inferno she wouldn't be able to put out.

Unless she did something drastic.

She'd had to stop the fire, and the only way she knew how was to "date" Ben.

She wasn't going to end up emotionally charred, her sanity reduced to ashes.

"Spencer ..." Shady prodded. "Tell us what happened ..."

9

San Ignacio, Belize
Belizean Banyan Resort — Owner's Casita

Once a sprawling plantation house in the 1800s, the casita where Sione lived, referred to as the Owner's Casita, had been the eleven-room vacation home of slave-owning sugar barons before it was bought by a Canadian couple who had repurposed it into a bed-and-breakfast.

A few years after Sione was born, his uncle bought the bed-and-breakfast, along with several acres of surrounding land, and began building resort casitas, marketing them toward travelers who wanted more privacy. Soon, more casitas were built, along with an Olympic-sized pool and a tennis court, and eventually, his uncle closed the bed-and-breakfast and turned it back into what it originally was, a large vacation home.

Frustrated with himself for forgetting the reports, Sione entered the casita, stepped into the expansive foyer, and then headed down the main hall, which bisected the two wings of the house.

A dozen or so feet from the foyer, a second hall ran perpendicular to the main hall, where a turn to the left would lead to the bedrooms, while a turn right led to the living areas, including the kitchen, dining room, and his casita office.

Once he turned right, a short walkway led to a labyrinth of more short hallways.

After turning several corners, Sione headed down a long hall.

At the end, a set of double doors led into his office, and he walked quickly toward them, checking his watch and thinking he might call the Front Desk, and ask one of the bellmen to get a golf cart to drive him back to the Administrative building.

Pushing open the door, he took a step and then stopped.

Confused and apprehensive, he stared toward his desk.

Last night's mistake, Karen, Kimberley, Kelsey, whatever the hell her damn name was, was on her knees in front of the small wooden file cabinet near the wall behind his desk, going through the bottom drawer, so intent on the files, she didn't seem to have heard him come in.

Well, he could fix that, he thought, and slammed the door.

Gasping, her head whipped toward him, and she leaped to her feet, stumbling slightly as she gaped at him, fear and chagrin clouding her green eyes.

"I thought you wanted to take a shower?" Sione walked toward her.

"I was just, um ..." she swallowed, stepping back, away from him. "I was looking for a pen and paper."

"In my file cabinet?"

"There were no blank sheets of paper on your desk." She swallowed and then said, "And I wanted to write you a note ..."

He took another step toward her. "A note?"

She took another step back and then said, "I wanted to leave you my number so maybe we could—"

"I don't want your number," he told her. "I want to know what the hell you're doing in my office."

"I told you," she said, backing up again, until she backed up against the edge of his desk. "I was going to—"

Jazz music cut her off, a breezy tone that made her jump, and her eyes darted toward the wooden file cabinet.

The swing tune was coming from a cell phone lying on top of the file cabinet.

"That's my phone," she told him, panic in her imploring gaze. "I need to get that …"

"You need to stay right where you are," he told her, stepping to the file cabinet and keeping his eyes on her, preparing himself for sudden movement. "Do not move …"

"But …" She glared at him, and he started to think of what he would do if she lunged at him. She had her dress on, but she was barefoot, so he wouldn't have to worry about having a stiletto stabbed in his eye. Her fingernails were another issue. Talons, actually, he thought, remembering the welts she'd scratched up and down his back. Even though he was head and shoulders above her, she was taller than most women, with longer arms, and she might be able to do some damage to his face.

"Don't move," he warned again, hoping she wouldn't try him.

Continuing to watch her, Sione grabbed the cell phone.

He glanced at the screen and determined that the jazz tone was the signal for a text message.

"Give me my phone," she told him, with enough command in her tone to make him wary. He would never hit a woman, but if she came at him, he would have to restrain her.

Deciding to put a bit more space between them, he walked across the room to the wall of bookshelves and looked at the screen again.

The text message she'd just received wasn't the only text.

There were several more, a chain of previous texts that sent a sliver of apprehension through him.

he's gone, now what?

gone for how long?

he's got meetings all day

have you found it? call me

He stared at her. "What the hell are you looking for? Who do you need to call?"

"Look," she said, cowering as she stood next to the desk, her eyes darting from him to the door and back to him. "Those messages have nothing to do with you."

"Answer my question." He decided to keep the distance between them, so he wouldn't be tempted to do something he might regret, like allow the anger simmering within him to take over and convince him to grab her and shake her until she gave him answers or he gave her brain damage, whichever came first.

"I knew this wasn't going to work!" She cursed and then dropped her face in her hands, mumbling incoherently.

Worried, Sione walked toward her. "You knew what wasn't going to work?"

Dragging her hands from her face and smearing mascara down her cheeks, she looked at him. "I told him this wasn't going to work. I told him I couldn't do this …"

"What the hell are you talking about?" Sione tossed her cell phone on his desk. "You told *who* you couldn't do *what*?"

"I told the man who forced me to help him that I would get caught!"

"I think you need to start from the beginning. Who the hell told you—"

"His name is Benjamin Chang," she said.

10

Houston, Texas
Moonlight Lake Apartments

"So, you think he found out that you stole his watches?" Shady asked when Spencer finished the story. "And that's why he shot at you?"

"That has to be why he tried to kill me," Spencer said. "I thought he was asleep. I thought I was being so careful and quiet, but—"

"But you should have drugged him," Rae cut in with her two cents, a rebuke Spencer wasn't in the mood for. "A few drops of GHB, and you wouldn't have been dodging bullets."

"Rae, don't be a bitch," Shady told her and then turned to Spencer. "I still can't believe you didn't get shot. Somehow, you jumped out of the way of that bullet. It's freaking amazing! God was protecting you."

"I guess." Spencer shrugged.

She wasn't so sure that God would save her life after she'd stolen money and watches, but maybe …

"My guess is the mofo can't handle a gun as well as Spencer

can use a knife," Rae said. "What I can't believe is that you stabbed Ben Chang and left the sonofabitch bleeding on the floor."

"I told you I didn't have a choice," Spencer countered, pissed at her older sister's tone, a mix of skepticism and condemnation.

Shady asked, "You think Ben is still alive?"

"I didn't kill him," Spencer said. "I mean, I don't ..."

Troubled, Spencer trailed off.

"You mean, you don't know if you killed him or not, do you?" Rae glared at her.

Spencer shook her head. "I don't think I did ..."

"It's not about what you think," Rae told her. "It's about what we gotta find out. We need to know for sure if the asshole is dead, or not."

"How are we gonna find out?" Shady asked.

"I'll ask Mr. Cephas," Rae said. "He knows cops. He can find out."

Mr. Cephas was Rae's fence, a disbarred attorney who now made a living on the wrong side of the law, often exploiting legal technicalities to keep his criminal enterprise seemingly legitimate.

A former friend of Rae's mother, Mr. Cephas was dedicated to protecting Rae, as evidenced by the fact that he'd hired one of the best criminal defense attorneys in the country to represent Rae when she'd been wrongly accused of a double homicide almost two years ago.

But their relationship was strange and complex.

Sometimes Mr. Cephas was like a father figure to Rae, and other times, he seemed to want to be her lover. As a result, their interactions had a weird, quasi-incestuous vibe that made Spencer feel uncomfortable and suspicious.

"You think we should get him involved?" Spencer asked, wary.

"Hell, yes, we need to get Mr. Cephas involved," Rae said. "If

Ben is dead, then you need to get a lawyer, because unlike me, you ain't innocent."

Wincing at Rae, Shady said, "Spencer, Mr. Cephas can get you a good lawyer, if you need one, and you probably won't."

Nodding, Spencer grabbed the mimosa with trembling hands and finished it off in one long, swallow.

"Shady's right," Rae said. "You probably didn't kill him, but just in case you did …"

Panicked and slightly queasy from chugging the mimosa, Spencer stared down toward the parking lot, focusing on the collection of cars, trucks, and SUVs.

More sun had forced its way between the low clouds and was glinting off windshields and candy-colored custom paint jobs, one of which was a large depiction of the Virgin Mary on the hood of a Chevy Impala.

Spencer didn't pray much, but she was hoping to God that she hadn't killed Ben.

And it wasn't that she was afraid about being charged with his murder, she just didn't want Ben to be dead.

He'd shot at her, and she'd stabbed him, but there was a part of her, a crazy, ridiculous, unrealistic part that still had feelings for him …

"Don't take this the wrong way," Rae started, her tone conspiratorial as she glanced from Spencer to Shady. "But it might not be so bad if you did kill Ben …"

"Are you out of your mind?" Spencer's heart took off, and she was tempted to slap her older sister.

"Rae …" Shady admonished. "Why would you say something like that?"

"If Ben Chang is alive," Rae started, "then you know he's pissed that Spencer stabbed him, and you know he's gonna come after her."

"Maybe he won't try to kill her again," Shady said, a note of wistful hope in her tone. "Maybe he'll give Spencer a chance to explain."

"Explain what?" Rae's voice rose in disbelief. "How the hell is she supposed to explain that she stole two Rolex watches from him?"

"She can tell Ben that she didn't mean to steal from him," Shady said. "And as a show of good faith, she can give the watches back to him, and maybe they can find a way to put this whole terrible misunderstanding behind them. And maybe Ben will remember how much he cares about Spencer, and he'll be in the mood to forgive her."

Spencer didn't know if she could agree with Shady or not.

She wanted to believe that Ben might be able to understand that she'd been confused and terrified when she'd stabbed him, and she hoped he might forgive her, but she wasn't counting on it.

"Shady, just shut up, okay?" Rae told her. "You always trying to give people the benefit of the doubt, but Ben Chang doesn't deserve it. That sonofabitch tried to kill our sister!"

"Because our sister stole from him," Shady countered, not backing down. "Which was something she didn't have to do, and something she never ever would have thought to do if …"

Shady trailed off, but Spencer knew what she'd been about to say.

Rae knew, too, because her gray eyes narrowed, and the furrow between her brows deepened. "Something she never would have thought to do if … what, Shady? What the hell were you going to say?"

Shady shook her head, looking away. "Nothing. It doesn't matter."

But now, Rae wasn't backing down. "No, Shady, I think it does matter—"

A faint chime drifted through the patio screen, which Rae had left closed after she'd pushed the glass partition back, in case the phone rang.

Spencer froze, and from the wary, wide-eyed looks on her sisters' faces, she had a feeling they'd gone numb, too, most likely for the same reason she had.

Finding her voice, Spencer asked, "You think it's the cops? You think they know I stabbed Ben, and they came to arrest me?"

"How would they know you're here?" Rae asked, starting to thaw.

"Maybe the cops went to Spencer's apartment, and when she wasn't there, they came here," Shady whispered. "Remember, Rae, when the cops thought you'd killed Karl and his wife, they followed me and Spencer, looking for you."

Swallowing, Spencer said, "The cops always check with a suspect's family members and friends."

Rolling her eyes, Rae stood. "Well, if it is the cops, I ain't gotta open the door, so ..."

After Rae went inside, Shady turned to Spencer. "Listen, I don't care what Rae said, I hope you didn't kill Ben. I hope he's still alive."

Spencer glared at her. "If he's alive, he's going to come after me, and maybe he'll succeed in killing me."

"But if he's dead, the cops will find out, and you'll get arrested, and you'll probably have to do some time." Shady sighed. "Jail could be worse than Ben coming after you."

"I don't know about that."

"Okay, if Ben is alive, he'll probably try to find you," Shady said. "But maybe by the time he does, he won't be so upset with you, and you can talk to him. You can tell him that you never meant to steal from him."

"Who says I didn't mean to steal from him?" Spencer snapped, staring at her empty glass. "He won't believe that."

"I think he'll listen to you," Shady said. "Because I know he cares about you. I remember when the three of us went to lunch, and you introduced him to me. He kept holding your hand and gazing at you adoringly."

"Shady, stop it," Spencer said, disgruntled, not in the mood to remember how she'd felt that day, so cherished and protected. "He was not gazing adoringly. And he's not going to care that I deeply regret my thoughtless actions."

"Just be honest," Shady suggested. "Tell him the truth."

"What truth?" Spencer asked. "That I'm a lying, thieving—"

"That's not who you are, okay?"

"What the hell are you talking about?" Spencer stared at her younger sister, wondering if Shady had lost her mind. "That's exactly what I am, Shady. I drug men, and I steal from them—"

"Listen, all maladaptive behavior—"

"Maladaptive behavior?"

"Negative choices," Shady clarified. "People make negative choices to reinforce negative ideals they believe about themselves."

"You need to stop watching Oprah."

"No, listen to me," Shady said. "It's like, if you think you're a bad person, then you'll do bad things to prove yourself right. Does that make sense?"

"Not really."

Frowning, Shady said, "What you think about yourself determines your actions, and if you think you're a lying thief, then you're going to lie and steal, so you have to change the way you think about yourself."

"And how the hell am I supposed to do that?" Spencer asked. "Right now, my head is a mess. I can barely focus! You can't expect me to 'think positively' or whatever the hell. The only thing I'm thinking about is, did I kill Ben? Or did he survive? If he's alive, will he come after me and kill me? If he's dead, are the cops going to figure out that I stabbed him and arrest me?"

Shady sighed and then glanced up as Rae returned to the

patio, holding a gift, the size of a shoebox, wrapped in elegant silver paper with a red velvet bow.

"What's that?" Shady asked, curious excitement in her gaze.

"Don't know …" Rae put the gift on the table and then sat. "But it ain't ticking, so …"

"Open it," Spencer told her, desperate to focus on something else besides the mess she'd made of her life.

Sighing, Rae lifted the top and set it aside. "I don't even know who sent it, and the delivery guy just shrugged when I asked him. He don't give a shit."

"Was there a card?" Spencer asked, eyeing Shady's untouched mimosa, which she knew her younger sister wouldn't drink, since alcohol was against her religion or something.

"If there was," Rae said, "the delivery dude didn't have it, or he probably lost it."

Grabbing Shady's drink, Spencer said, "Well, don't keep us in suspense."

Shrugging, Rae looked into the box and then frowned.

"What is it?" Shady asked.

A second later, Rae screamed.

11

San Ignacio, Belize
Belizean Banyan Resort — Owner's Casita

"Do you know him?" Kelsey, the mistake, asked. "Benjamin Chang?"

Sione knew him.

Too damn well, but he could not let this woman know that. He couldn't tell anyone just how well he knew Ben Chang.

And nobody could know how much Ben knew him better than anyone else did. He knew things about Sione that no one could ever know, all the secrets he fought to keep hidden, secrets that could destroy and dismantle the life Sione had tried to create.

Sione said, "I've heard of him ..."

The truth was, he and Ben Chang had grown up together and had once been closer than brothers, raised by the same man, and taught the same dangerous lessons.

But that changed when Sione's uncle had stepped in and rescued him from that life.

"Is he, um ..." Kelsey took another deep breath. "Is he dangerous?"

"Dangerous?"

Ben Chang was more than dangerous. He was an unpre-
dictable foe, an undefeatable adversary.

"He told me not to cross him," she said. "He told me I would
be sorry if I tried."

"He's definitely not the kind of guy you want to be mixed up
with," Sione decided to say. "How do you know him?"

"It's a long story."

"I have time."

"No, you don't," she said. "You have a meeting you can't be
late for."

"It's okay. I know the owner. He won't mind me being late,"
he told her. "Now tell me how you know Ben Chang."

"I made the mistake of asking him for help," she said. "I own
a souvenir shop in Jamaica, and last year, business wasn't so
great, and I got behind on my mortgage, and it got to the point
where the bank was threatening to foreclose, and ..."

She trailed off and dropped her face in her hands again. Sione
gave her a chance to collect herself and didn't force her to
continue.

He didn't need to ...

He'd heard her story before, two years ago.

The details were slightly different, but the end of the story
would be the same.

Ben Chang uses threats and blackmail to force the beautiful
girl to do his bidding, and things run smoothly for a while, until
they don't, and when everything goes to hell, the girl takes the
blame, and Ben gets away.

His uncle had always told him, the devil don't have no new
tricks.

"And so," Kelsey sighed and then went on, "Ben agreed to
help me out, he paid off the mortgage, and things went back to
normal, business picked up. But then he asked me for a favor. He
said he'd met a woman who made beautiful glass menagerie

figures, and he wanted to sell them in my shop, and I didn't think I could say no, not after he'd saved my business.

"So ... the menagerie didn't sell very well. I moved maybe one or two pieces every other week," she said. "But Ben kept sending more shipments of it, even though I told him it wasn't selling. And the weird thing was, whenever a shipment came in, Ben would have one of his associates unload it. Now, these were fairly large-sized boxes, but Ben's associate would unload three or four menagerie figures, and menagerie is usually very small."

"Did you ask the associate about that?" Sione asked, though he knew where the story was headed.

Kelsey nodded. "He told me that because the figurines were so small and delicate, extra care was taken to ship them, and they quadrupled the amount of packing so that the figurines wouldn't break during shipping."

"Did you believe him?"

"No, I didn't," she admitted. "And then one day, a shipment came, and Ben's associate was delayed. So, I opened the boxes—"

"I don't want to hear any more," he told her. "All I want to know is, where is Ben Chang right now? Is he in Belize?"

"I think so." Kelsey nodded. "When I arrived a few days ago, he sent someone to pick me up from the airport, and the guy took me to a house right outside of San Ignacio, a pretty nice place, really big."

Nodding, Sione said, "Yeah, I know."

"You've been there?" Kelsey asked, the slight suspicion in her green-eyed gaze again.

Sione stared at her, kicking himself for the slip. "I've heard about it. Look, tell me this. Our little chance encounter last night wasn't exactly a chance encounter, was it?"

Looking down, Kelsey shook her head.

"Ben Chang told you to ... what?"

"He wanted me to get close to you."

"And then what?"

Rubbing her arms, she was hesitant to look at him. "The goal was for me to get into your casita, but I couldn't break in. He was really adamant about that. No forced entry. I had to get myself invited into your casita, or I had to trick my way in, and then I had to find some way to get you out of the casita so I could ..."

"So you could what?"

"I was supposed to steal your passport," Kelsey said, sighing. "So, after you left, I checked around in your bedroom and didn't find it, so I made my way through the house and found your office, so I decided to look in here, in your file cabinet."

Skeptical, Sione stared at her. "Ben told you to steal my passport?"

He wasn't sure if he believed her or not.

One of Ben's money laundering scams involved the use of passports, but usually, the passports weren't stolen, they belonged to the stable of "mules" he used as couriers to smuggle for him.

Nodding, she said, "He told me that he'd give me the next step after I found your passport."

"The next step?"

"He said the favor would be a series of steps," Kelsey said. "And I wouldn't find out the next step until I had successfully completed the previous step."

"And you completed the first step?"

"Yes," she told him. "Step One was to get close to you, and Step Two was to get myself alone in your casita and find your passport. And Step Three ... I don't know, because I didn't get to call him."

Sighing, Sione said, "But you should, or he might get suspicious."

Panic etched on her face, creating lines of worry, and she said, "But I haven't found your passport."

"No, you haven't," he said, then walked to his desk, and picked up her phone.

"I can't tell him that," she said, pushing away from the desk and taking a few staggering steps toward him. "I have to do this favor for him. He told me not to disappoint him, or ..."

Kelsey trailed off, interrupted by more tears.

Sione knew what would happen to her. He knew she'd suffer the same fate that another beautiful, desperate woman had suffered. She would find out what happened when you got on the bad side of Ben Chang.

"If I don't do this favor," Kelsey said, "I will lose everything."

"You lost everything when you went to Ben Chang for help," he told her. "You already know that was your worst mistake."

Tears streaming down her cheeks, she whispered, "What am I supposed to do?"

"Another favor," Sione said. "But for me this time."

Wary, she glanced up at him. "What kind of favor?"

"I want you to call Ben," Sione said. "Tell him you found my passport, and ask him what he wants you to do next ..."

San Ignacio, Belize
Belizean Banyan Resort – Owner's Casita

In his casita office, Sione yanked the middle desk drawer out as far as it could go.

He stared at the beige square of chamois cloth, hesitating.

A month had passed since his encounter with Kelsey, the mistake that had turned into a nightmare when she'd revealed that their hook-up hadn't been random, after all, but orchestrated, one of the steps in some bizarre plan.

A plan Sione still didn't understand or have any answers about.

Ben Chang had put the plan in motion, but his end game remained a mystery.

Kelsey had agreed to help Sione figure out what Ben was up to, but when she'd called Ben, the son of a bitch hadn't answered.

After two days of attempting to contact Ben, Kelsey gave up and left the country, and Sione hadn't heard anything from her.

But last night, a friend in Montego Bay had called him and

told him Kelsey had been arrested and charged with drug trafficking and money laundering.

Sione couldn't help but blame himself.

He'd known what Ben Chang had planned for Kelsey, and he was convinced that things might have turned out differently for her if he had ... what?

What the hell could he have done?

By the time Kelsey had turned to him for guidance, it was already too late, and no amount of remorseful tears would change the fact that there would be hell to pay.

Ben Chang was a guy who wanted something in exchange for his assistance, and usually, that something was illegal, and if he didn't get what he wanted, there would be dangerous consequences.

Kelsey had been screwed the moment she asked Ben for help.

Just like his ex-fiancée, another woman who'd been stupid enough to trust that Ben Chang wanted to take care of her and had her best interest at heart.

Two years ago, Sione's ex had come to him, desperate and crying, and when she'd begged him to help her, he couldn't refuse, though he had every right to tell her to kiss his ass.

But her heaving sobs damn near broke his heart, and Sione had tried to get her out of trouble.

Things hadn't gone as he'd planned.

Now, his ex blamed him for her misfortune and held him responsible for Ben's deceptive attack against her. A year ago, during their last, and possibly final, conversation, she'd been bitter and accusatory.

"You let this happen to me, Sione," she'd sneered, glaring at him from behind thick, scratched, and smudged Plexiglas, gripping the phone they were forced to communicate through. "You wanted to get back at me for what I did to you ..."

No amount of protest on his part would sway her.

To this day, she remained convinced that he'd been harboring secret hatred toward her and was dead set on getting his revenge.

Sione ran his fingers across the smooth chamois.

It was true that she'd hurt him. Their relationship had been ruined because of her stupid, selfish choices, and for a while, he did feel bitter and resentful toward her.

But a part of him was also relieved that the relationship had ended.

She wasn't the woman for him, he realized, and not just because she'd proved to be a lying bitch. Even before she'd betrayed him, he'd begun to believe asking her to marry him had been a mistake.

But he'd never wanted her to end up paying a terrible price for something she hadn't done. He hated the idea of her spending the next twenty years behind bars and hated that her days were wasted in a dirty prison where disease, corruption, and danger ran rampant.

The last time he'd seen her, she had still been beautiful, but the bitterness behind her eyes spoiled the delicate features that had guaranteed her success in beauty pageants across the globe.

Sometimes, he blamed himself for her vengeful, vacant gaze, and he wondered if she was right, if somehow subconsciously, he'd failed her on purpose.

Often, guilt over his botched attempt to keep his ex-fiancée out of jail would grab hold of him, as if in a death grip or that chokehold maneuver he'd perfected.

More than once, he'd thought of how he might rectify the situation, how he might find a way to get his ex released from prison, but the answers to her freedom remained hidden from him.

Sione lifted the cloth, revealing a formidable weapon, a destructive, bloody connection to his past.

A set of steel knuckles studded with four real tiger's claws.

The claws had been given to him by his father, Richard Tuiali'i, for a specific purpose, one Sione had never been able to fulfill ...

The black, four-inch razor-sharp claws, capable of ripping a man's throat out with one deadly slash, had been stolen from a real tiger. Hunted and killed by poachers, the animal had been hacked to pieces, each one sold to the highest bidder. Richard had risked his life and his freedom to get those claws. They'd come at a high price and with grim expectations.

The claws always reminded Sione of the night when he was supposed to have proven that the lessons he'd learned from Richard hadn't been in vain.

Sione had made promises to his father that night, but he hadn't been able to keep them.

He and Ben were going to do the job together.

They had followed the guy they were looking for and set a simple ambush, one the man hadn't noticed and had easily stumbled into. Before Sione had realized it, Ben had grabbed the man and yanked the man's head backward, revealing his bare throat...

Sione had stared at the exposed skin, the Adam's apple bobbing up and down as the man swallowed reflexively, and Sione's stomach had lurched and his hands had shook.

"What you waiting on ..." Ben growled in a whisper. "Come on, do it ... we ain't got all night ..."

But, Sione could do nothing except back away, feeling sick and faint, and he had opened his mouth to tell Ben that he couldn't do it, but no words came.

Ben had whispered more angry commands, but Sione had stood still, frozen.

Cursing, Ben had hit the man several times, wrestling him to the ground where he had kicked him half-unconscious. Then he had stalked over to Sione, and yanked the tiger claws from Sione's trembling hand, damn near breaking his fingers in the process ...

With the tiger claws, Ben went back to the man, took a knee next to him, and—

Sione forced the memory from his mind, and then dropped down in the leather chair, staring at the tiger claws.

Why had he taken them from their normal hiding place, the bottom drawer of his wardrobe in the closet? What the hell did he plan to do with them? He wasn't sure, but he felt like he might need them. For protection, possibly.

Tonight, especially.

He'd been thinking about paying a visit to Ben Chang since he'd found out that Ben was staying at his residence in Maya Vista.

Ben's plan, with its orchestrated steps, had distracted Sione since the news about Kelsey's arrest, and he'd made up his mind that he had to find out what the hell kind of attack Ben was about to launch against him.

He couldn't sit around speculating, trying to second-guess Ben.

He had to know for sure what kind of hell Ben was trying to unleash.

And, if possible, he had to stop all hell from breaking loose, but not with the claws.

Sione stood, hesitating again.

The claws were one of the last shackles to the life he'd once lived, the life he'd left behind, and he should have gotten rid of them long ago. He wasn't sure why he hadn't, and maybe he didn't want to know, but right now, he was torn.

The claws were designed for destruction, and if he had to use them, for whatever reason, the end result would be mangled and bloody.

Which was why he knew he couldn't take them.

He had to rely on what he knew was right, not what he'd been taught.

Leaving his office, the tiger's claws once again wrapped in the chamois cloth, Sione headed to his bedroom. He would put the claws back where they belonged. He didn't need them.

The claws would give him an option for violence that he couldn't take.

An option he might not be able to resist.

13

Houston, Texas
El Nino's Tex-Mex Cantina

"Hey, girl," Rae said, sliding into the booth, her gray eyes mischievous. "What's up?"

Across the table, Spencer glared at her sister. "Where the hell have you been? My lunch break is only an hour, and I've wasted twenty minutes of it waiting for you to get here!"

This morning, while Spencer was getting ready to go to work, Rae had called, asking to meet her for lunch, and said she had something to tell her. It was important and they had to talk in person.

Reluctantly, Spencer had agreed.

She had a feeling she knew what Rae wanted to talk about.

Her older sister wanted her to start "dating" again, and Spencer wasn't in the mood for another hard sell, which Rae had begun doing less than a week after the nightmare Spencer had barely survived at Ben Chang's townhouse.

It was now a month later, and Rae was getting on her last

damn nerve, trying to pressure her into "dating," but Spencer had made up her mind.

She was never "dating" again.

And to prove it, she'd joined a temp agency and had recently gotten an assignment at a wealth management company that had the potential to become permanent. Hopefully. So far, things were going okay. She'd made a few mistakes, nothing too drastic, nothing that had gotten her fired. Yet. But it was a male-dominated office, and she could tell the men liked having her around.

Sometimes, their lingering glances made her wary.

And when she saw them walk out to their expensive European sedans, sly thoughts would sneak into her head. How easy would it be to go out for a drink with the dirty old goats? Once or twice, she'd been invited to happy hour. How easy would it be to target one of the dirty goats and suggest they break away from the herd for a more private conversation? And when she and the old goat were alone in his ginormous Memorial mansion, with his wife away shopping in Paris, how easy would it be to make him a drink, put a few drops of GHB in it, and then—

Too damn easy, Spencer knew.

And probably very lucrative. Most of the old goats wore one-hundred-thousand-dollar watches, and Rae's fence could probably get half that amount, but …

Spencer was never going to "date" again.

Rae smiled as she settled herself on the bench seat, placing her purse on the table.

It was a classic, quilted Chanel that Spencer hadn't seen before, and Spencer suspected was stolen from one of her sister's recent "dates."

"The reason I was late is because I'm baking a pie tonight," Rae said, thanking the waitress who sat a tall glass of water in front of her and then walked away to give them more time to peruse the menu. "And I had to buy apples."

Tensing, Spencer stared at the plastic menu, her appetite

quickly diminishing despite the fact that moments ago she'd been ravenous.

She'd skipped breakfast, and work had been slow since three of the partners were out of town. Spencer was looking forward to nachos slathered in cheese and greasy chorizo and topped with pico de gallo, one of the cantina's specialties.

But Rae's sly, inside reference to "dating" had her stomach churning.

Baking pie and buying apples was secret "dating" code that only the two of them understood and couldn't possibly be decoded by anyone who happened to overhear, or who perhaps might be listening on purpose.

Baking pie and buying apples meant that Rae had lined up a "date" for Spencer.

In the past, when Spencer had been actively "dating," she'd found her own old farts to fleece, but sometimes, Rae would meet a guy, and instead of "dating" him herself, she would pass him along to Spencer.

Normally, these men were rich and close to death, easy to make fools of.

Rae referred to them as "apples" because the thought of kissing them would make you turn Granny Smith green.

"Have you been to this place before?" Rae picked up the menu, decorated with colorful cartoon versions of jalapeños, sombreros, and mariachis. "What's good here?"

"The apple pie is terrible," Spencer told her.

Rae pursed her lips and then said, "Girl, what is your problem? You know you need the money."

Spencer was about to reply, but the waitress came back with a bowl of complimentary tortilla chips and salsa and then took their orders.

After the waitress took their menus and walked away, Spencer said, "I don't need the money that bad. I told you, I am not interested in apple pie, and I never will be interested again."

"So, what are you gonna do?" Rae sat back, crossing her arms. "Work temp jobs for the rest of your life? You can't pay the bills on fifteen dollars an hour."

"Why can't you understand that after what happened with Ben—"

"Forget about Ben Chang." Rae leaned forward, her gray eyes fierce. "What did I tell you last week? Mr. Cephas' contact at HPD told him that Ben is still alive, he went to the hospital that night, and he told the ER doctors that he'd been mugged, and he didn't see who did it, so you ain't gotta worry about going to jail."

Rae was right about that.

Mr. Cephas' news had been a relief, a burden lifted.

But a nagging worry persisted, one Spencer couldn't identify. A wariness she couldn't ignore cautioned her against thinking that all was well and she was free to go about her life without the threat of any reprisal from Ben.

"Okay, listen," Rae said. "If you had a murder rap hanging over your head, then yeah, I would see why you wouldn't be interested in apple pie. But you're in the clear. Obviously, the mofo is not going to rat you out, so you don't have to worry."

"But what if I do?"

Eyes narrowed, Rae asked, "What are you talking about?"

"Don't you think it's strange that Ben didn't tell the cops what I did?" Spencer asked, looking for corroboration of her suspicions. "Don't you wonder why he didn't?"

Rae grabbed a chip and dunked it into the salsa. "Not really."

"Well, I do," Spencer said. "I think there's a reason why he didn't tell the police and why he lied to the ER doctors about what happened to him."

After Rae ate the salsa-laden chip, she said, "The reason is that he likes you, and he didn't want you to go to jail."

"I don't think so."

At least, Spencer hoped it wasn't so. She hoped that Ben's

reasons for not telling the cops she'd robbed him and then stabbed him had nothing to do with his feelings for her.

Because that didn't make any sense.

Ben had tried to kill her that night.

He'd put a gun in her face and pulled the trigger because he'd found out that she'd stolen his money and watches.

She couldn't believe that he would forgo the chance to make her pay for her crimes because he had fallen for her, or whatever.

"Ben still wants you," Rae went on, grabbing another chip. "Just like you still want him."

"Who the hell says I still want Ben Chang?" Spencer asked. "Who says I ever wanted him?"

"Don't lie to me," Rae warned, pointing a tortilla chip at Spencer. "I saw y'all together, remember? Holding hands and smiling at each other at the Chanel store in the Galleria? You tried to pretend you didn't know who I was, and you only introduced me to him because I forced you to."

"I didn't pretend I didn't know you," Spencer said, rolling her eyes.

"Whatever." Rae waved her hand. "The point is, Ben Chang is good-looking and rich and you know you like him."

"I don't like Ben," Spencer told her. "I mean, I don't really like *him*. I just liked that he took me out to nice restaurants and I didn't have to pay."

It wasn't entirely true. That wasn't all she liked about Ben Chang.

The nice restaurants weren't even on the top ten list.

She'd liked Ben's companionship and compassion; he made her feel like she mattered to him; and while he appreciated her beauty, he didn't define her by her looks.

"That's not all you liked," Rae said, a bit too sly.

"Whatever, the fact remains, I'm not interested in apple pie," Spencer said, anxious to change the subject. "But I am interested in that gift you got last month …"

"I'm not worried about it." Rae rolled her eyes. "And you shouldn't be either."

"But did you even find out who sent it?" Spencer shivered a bit, remembering what had been inside the beautifully wrapped package.

Rae dropped the chip she'd been about to eat, then grabbed her water, and took a long sip.

"You know, I don't even think it was for me," she said. "There wasn't a card, and that delivery guy didn't seem like he gave a damn. He probably took it to the wrong address."

"You don't know that for sure," Spencer told her. "What does Mr. Cephas think you should do?"

Rae took another sip of water and then shrugged. "I didn't tell him."

Spencer was shocked. "Why not? If anybody could find out who sent that—"

"Look, I just didn't tell him, okay?" Rae said. "I don't want to get him in the middle of it."

"In the middle of ... what?" Spencer asked, realizing there was something Rae wasn't telling her and something was bothering Rae. Spencer could tell by the strange furtiveness in her sister's eyes.

"Nothing," Rae snipped. "Don't worry about it."

"Well, I am worried."

"Don't be," Rae snapped and then relaxed her scowl when, moments later, the waitress came to their table with an order of sizzling fajitas they planned to share.

When the waitress was gone, Spencer said, "Maybe you should call the cops about that gift."

"Are you out of your damn mind?" Rae growled. "The cops won't give a shit, okay? Most of them still believe that I killed Karl and his wife—"

"No charges were filed against you," Spencer reminded her,

leaning back to avoid the onion-and-pepper scented smoke wafting from the grilled beef.

"The D.A. didn't file charges because they didn't have enough evidence," Rae said. "It wasn't because they thought I didn't kill Karl. It was because they couldn't prove I did it."

Spencer sighed. "I still think—"

"I don't care what you think," Rae said, stabbing her fork into a hunk of meat. "Just forget about that gift, okay?"

Her appetite returning somewhat, Spencer put a strip of beef on her plate and then added a few grilled onions. "It's kind of hard to forget—"

"I mean it, Spencer," Rae said, pointing the fork at her. "Forget about the gift, and especially, forget about what you saw inside …"

Rae trailed off, staring at something behind Spencer, several emotions racing across her face, apprehension, panic, and anger.

"What is it?" Spencer asked.

Rae looked down and began assembling a fajita, grabbing a tortilla and placing the beef in the middle. Her hands trembled as she added cheese, pico de gallo, and jalapeños.

"What is it?" Spencer leaned over the table, her voice lowered. "Are you okay—"

"Why the hell haven't you returned any of my calls?"

Startled by the deep, masculine voice, Spencer turned her head and looked up.

Standing next to their booth was a tall guy dressed in a dark suit that couldn't hide his muscles, and he was handsome enough to never be ignored.

But Rae was doing just that, adding more cheese to the mound of shredded Colby jack she'd already heaped upon the beef.

"Desarae," the guy said, glaring down at Rae.

And yet, Spencer had a feeling his anger came from some concern, not ire, and she wondered who the hell he was and how he knew her sister? What was their connection, and why hadn't Rae mentioned this incredible hunk before?

With a furious exhale, Rae looked up at him. "Maybe I'm not returning your calls because I don't want to talk to you."

"Look, I understand that you're pissed at me," the guy said. "But, we need to discuss that *gift* you got, because—"

"Not here …" Rae cut him off, grounding the words through gritted teeth. "Okay?"

Spencer glanced at her sister, who was trying to avoid looking at her, and then at the guy, whose intense stare was focused on Rae.

Again, she wondered who the hell was this guy?

And how did he know about the gift Rae had gotten? Had Rae told him? And why did he and Rae need to discuss the gift? What the hell was going on between them?

"Then where?" the guy asked.

"I'll text you," Rae said, giving him an evil side eye.

"When?" the guy asked, dubious.

"Tonight."

"You promise?" he asked, a gruff tenderness in his voice that made Rae's features soften, and when her sister glanced at the guy again, there was an emotion in her gray eyes that looked a lot like affection, and maybe even longing.

But Spencer wasn't sure, because the emotion that had replaced the hostile tension between them dissipated, and skepticism and mistrust returned.

Rolling her eyes, Rae said, "Yeah, I promise."

Spencer thought the guy still looked suspicious, and she sensed his reluctance to leave, but eventually, he walked away.

"Don't ask," Rae warned when the guy was gone. "Please, just … don't ask."

14

San Ignacio, Belize
Maya Vista

Sione turned off the main highway and onto a private road cut through a copse of banyan and banana trees, headlights illuminating the brush and trees and wide, green leaves.

Gripping the steering wheel, he drove up the winding dirt path toward the gravel driveway fronting a large plantation-style home.

Ben Chang's Belizean residence.

Parking beneath the portico, Sione cut the engine and hesitated.

More than once as he'd driven to the house, he'd allowed his mind to float into the future, trying to predict what would happen when he finally saw Ben Chang again.

The last time had been two years ago, and things had ended badly.

Reluctant, Sione stepped out of the car, and the smell of damp earth from the afternoon thundershower greeted him.

The atmosphere was familiar, the dusk wrapping around him

like an old, scratchy blanket, while above him, the hazy royal blue sky seemed to be descending upon him, intent on swallowing him in the inky blackness that would follow as night prevailed.

By the time he'd reached the ornate, wrought iron double door, he was struggling to fight the panic and apprehension.

Something about the twilight took him back almost ten years, to another time, another night, when he'd ventured out into the dusk.

It had rained that day, too, and when the sun had set, the humidity and smell of damp earth had clung to his skin, feeling like something growing along the surface and adding to his discomfort, his fear, and his reluctance ...

Back then, he'd been afraid and embarrassed, scared of what would be thought of him if he didn't deliver on the promises he'd made, if he didn't go through with what was expected of him.

Tonight, he was worried what might happen if he didn't find out why the hell Ben had blackmailed a woman to get close to him so she could be alone in his casita.

That woman, Kelsey Thomas, was now sitting in a Jamaican jail cell, waiting to be tried on drug trafficking charges.

At this point, the most Sione could do was find a good defense attorney to represent her, which he had done, even though his cousin Truman had advised him against getting involved.

Initially, Sione had wanted to post her bond, but bail had been denied due to the seriousness of her multiple indictments.

Truman had advised him against that, too.

"You don't even know this girl. Who is she?" Truman had asked as Sione walked alongside him, heading down a path through large Banyan trees, on their way to one of the resort restaurants. "Some skank you met at a club and then took home? Why the hell do you have to find her a lawyer?"

"She's in a lot of trouble," Sione said. "She needs help."

"There you go," Truman tsked. "Trying to be the hero again."

Truman's not so subtle reference to Sione's botched attempt

to keep his ex-fiancée out of prison pissed Sione off, but he let it slide, and instead had insisted he wasn't trying to be heroic, just compassionate, like his uncle Siosi, who had encouraged him to help those that were less fortunate.

"Your uncle was talking about the poor, the sick, the needy," Truman countered. "Not some drug dealing bitch."

At that point, Sione had given up trying to make Truman understand.

Sione hardly understood himself.

He wasn't trying to be Kelsey's hero, but when he thought about what Ben had done to her and he remembered her desperate tears and her fear, Sione felt guilty, and he couldn't stop wondering if he could have done more to help her.

When he'd met Kelsey in that club a month ago, she'd been smiling and vivacious, and remembering her grass green eyes, he wondered if prison would render them vacant and bitter.

There had to be some way to stop Ben, to make sure he never capitalized on the hidden weaknesses of another beautiful woman, or used blackmail and manipulation to exploit and abuse some woman who thought the son of a bitch cared about her.

What Sione wanted to do was find a way to prove that his ex-fiancée and Kelsey had been framed. He wanted to prove Ben had set them up to take the fall for crimes he'd committed.

Then maybe his ex-fiancée would stop hating him.

And maybe he could finally atone for the mistake he'd made when he'd let Ben get away.

15

San Ignacio, Belize
Maya Vista

"Sione ..." Ben Chang stepped back and allowed Sione to enter the foyer. "Old friend ..."

Forcing himself not to hesitate, Sione walked through the door, shoulder checking Ben, an action he'd done on purpose to let Ben know he wasn't there for a chat between old acquaintances.

"Why do you want to get close to me?" Sione turned. "What the hell are you up to?"

"What are you talking about?" Ben closed the door and then headed through the wide entryway into the study. "I know better than to try to get close to you. Didn't you tell me to stay the hell away from you? When you told me that you didn't want me in your life because you had changed, I respected your wishes."

Frustrated, Sione shook his head and followed him.

He'd asked the wrong damn question. He'd phrased it wrong and had given Ben a chance to dredge up a hostile moment from the past, when Ben had reached out to him, wanting them to again be the "brothers" Richard had raised them to be.

Ben had wanted them to be friends again, like they once were.

But Sione had burned all the bridges that lead to Ben Chang and that old way of life because he'd had to, not necessarily because he'd wanted to.

Ben was like a brother to him, and Sione supposed the hints of camaraderie and brotherly affection he felt in Ben's presence would always tempt him, but he couldn't go back to that destructive life.

There was too much at stake.

Any association with Ben would be an invitation to partake in that diabolical mayhem that Richard had introduced them to, and Sione couldn't take any chances. He couldn't risk being taken in by those old lures.

"You know what I'm talking about," Sione said. "Remember Kelsey Thomas. You threatened her, told her she had to do a favor for you, which happened to be getting close to me so she could get herself alone in my casita."

"Kelsey Thomas …" Ben walked to the bamboo bar cabinet near the large window and poured rum into a glass. "You know, that name does sound familiar. I think I read something about her. Did she get arrested for drug smuggling?"

"You're a real cold-blooded son of a bitch," Sione told him. "Letting her take the blame for crimes you committed."

"She's lucky I didn't do worse to her." Ben took a few steps forward, sipping his drink and slipping a hand into the pocket of his slacks. "As far as I'm concerned, I saved her life, letting her take the fall. In prison, she'll be safe from me. You could say I did her a favor."

"You did her a favor?" Sione stared at him. "She's probably going to prison for the rest of her life because of you."

"Why are you so upset about Kelsey Thomas?" Ben said. "You don't even know the woman."

"I'm upset because you're pulling the same shit you pulled two years ago—"

"Now, I get it," Ben said, nodding. "Kelsey Thomas reminds you of your beauty queen, who also made the mistake of trying to cross me—"

"Trying to cross you? What the hell are you talking about, she was trying to stay out of jail," Sione said. "She found out you were setting her up, making it look like she was laundering money through her boutique."

"You still think your beauty queen was an innocent victim? You think she didn't know I was doing a little creative accounting and being creative with the inventory? You don't know a damn thing about who she really was—"

"What I know is that you tricked her and used her," Sione said. "You made her think you cared about her and she trusted you. But when she got suspicious, you cut her off at the knees—"

"She was not what you think, old friend," Ben said. "You know, it was her idea to create those fictitious super rich clients, those Chinese women with billionaire husbands who would call in orders and pay in cash—"

"That's not true," Sione said. "That's your scam."

"I wasn't the villain," Ben said. "That beauty queen was greedy and devious. She was stealing from me, which means she was stealing from my clients, men who knew my great grandfather and trusted me because of him. She could have gotten me killed, which would have started a war—"

"Fuck your Triad bullshit!" Sione told him.

Abruptly, Ben pitched the glass toward him, and Sione ducked, side-stepping.

Glass shattered and the heady scent of rum floated through the air as Ben lunged at Sione, crouched low, using his shoulder to ram into Sione's chest, driving him backward, out of the study and into the foyer.

Sione fought to stay on his feet, but lost his balance and hit the floor, struggling to get up as Ben grabbed him around the throat.

Grabbing Ben's wrist with his left hand, Sione tried to pull Ben's hand from his throat, then balled his right hand into a fist, and slammed it into Ben's gut. Ben tried like hell to keep him pinned to the floor, but Sione got to his knees and punched his fist into Ben's chest. Finally feeling the hold loosen a bit around his neck, Sione crashed his fist down against Ben's wrist, breaking the hold.

Ben reached for him again, but Sione hit him in the jaw, then drew back, and smashed his fist into his chin.

Ben caught him in the side, a vicious blow that reverberated up his spine, and when he staggered back, Ben grabbed him by the shoulders and head-butted him. Pain detonated behind his skull and Sione dropped to one knee.

Ben kicked him in the gut. Sione doubled over, his stomach pitching, and went to his hands and knees.

Ben's foot swung toward his face.

Sione grabbed Ben's ankle and yanked it. As Ben crashed to the floor, Sione crawled over to him, grabbed him by the neck of his shirt, and smashed his fist into the center of Ben's face.

Ben's head jerked back.

Sione punched him again and then once more, scraping his knuckles across Ben's teeth as he smashed his fist into his mouth again.

Ben's head lolled forward, blood dribbling over his lips, and then his head dipped back, revealing a cut above his right eye, bruised and swollen. Shaken, disturbed by how quickly the anger had gotten out of control, Sione pushed Ben away, then staggered to his feet, and stumbled over toward the side table.

Hands raw and bloody, clutching the edge of the table for support, Sione glanced up.

His own grisly image confronted him, condemned him.

Bruises on his cheek and on his chin, and a slight reddish swelling across his forehead.

Disgusted, he turned from the mirror, from the truth reflected at him, the person he really was …

Ben was sitting on the floor, breathing hard and staring at him.

"His own iniquities shall take the wicked himself, and he shall be holden with the cords of his sins …"

Sione stared at him. "What …?"

His smile lopsided, Ben wiped blood from his cut lip and then went on, "… he shall die without instruction, and in the greatness of his folly he shall go astray …"

"Really?" Sione shook his head. "You're going to quote the Bible to me?"

Grunting, Ben got to his feet. "Get the hell out of my house."

"I'm not leaving until you tell me why you sent Kelsey Thomas to get close to me."

"And if I don't tell you, then what? You'll kill me? Somehow, old friend, I don't think so. You had the chance to kill me, and you didn't do it, remember? If I recall correctly, you had your hands around my neck, but you didn't rip my throat out, like you were taught to do."

Sione stared at him, trying to control the anger.

"I always wanted Richard to show me how to do that, but he said no. He said that technique was something special, reserved just for you," Ben said. "Tell me something, how many times did you use it properly? Not just to scare or intimidate, but when did you use that technique for the purpose it was intended?"

"You know what, Ben," Sione said. "I should use that technique on you."

"Oh really?" He smiled.

"But I don't want to see you dead," Sione told him. "I want to see you suffer …"

"How long did it take you to come up with that?" Ben

laughed. "It does sound intimidating, and I might be afraid if I didn't know the truth about you. You don't want to see me dead because while you have the skills, you lack the fortitude and the courage. You don't have the guts to kill me."

"You think I don't?"

"You never have been able to get the job done."

It was a subtle insult, but Sione wasn't going to feel inadequate because he hadn't been able to take another life despite his promises.

"Like I said"—Sione took a deep breath—"I didn't come to kill you, or you would be dead right now."

"Promises, promises," Ben laughed. "You don't have the guts. You didn't have the guts that night, when you were supposed to prove yourself worthy of those tiger claws, and you don't have the guts now."

"I didn't come here to talk about that night."

"Of course, you didn't," Ben walked to the curving staircase and sat on the fourth step. "You don't ever want to talk about that night. You just want to forget it, don't you? Because it reminds you of what you are."

"And what is that?" Sione crossed his arms, trying to ignore the anger flaring within him again.

"A coward," Ben sighed. "And a liar. That night was supposed to be a test of your skills. I was just going along to be the confirming witness, but I had to—"

"We both know what you did," Sione told him. "And we both know why you were capable of doing it, because—"

"I did what you couldn't do!" Ben yelled. "You wanted to do it, but you couldn't, and still can't—"

"I'm going to do what I should have done two years ago," Sione told him. "I'm going to make sure that you spend the rest of your worthless life in jail."

Shaking his head, Ben laughed and then said, "How are you going to do that? You going to find some snitch to rat on me? You do that, and all you will have to show for your efforts is a dead rat."

Sione rubbed his eyes and told himself to focus, to remember why he was there.

He had to find out why Ben had wanted Kelsey Thomas to steal his passport, because he wasn't convinced that the reason had anything to do with what he'd originally thought. He didn't believe Ben wanted to use his passport in one of his money-laundering schemes.

"Why the hell did you tell Kelsey Thomas to steal my passport?" Sione asked.

Ben leaned forward, rested his elbows on his knees, and fixed Sione with a penetrating glare. "Stealing your passport was a test."

"What kind of test?"

"A test to see if she would be able to find what I really wanted her to look for."

"And what the hell did you really want her to look for in my casita?"

Heart slamming, Sione waited, wondering what the hell Ben was going to tell him, not sure he wanted to know.

"Something your father wants," Ben said, his smile more like a taunting sneer.

Confused and numb, Sione stared at Ben, trying to wrap his mind around what Ben was telling him, trying to figure it out, but it didn't make sense.

"And if you want to know what he wants," Ben said. "Then you will have to ask your father."

16

Houston, Texas
Randall's Grocery Store

Spencer Edwards pushed her empty grocery basket into the produce section, navigating through the maze of bins piled high with fresh fruit and vegetables.

At eleven p.m. on a Thursday night in August, the sprawling, cavernous store was practically deserted, with only a skeleton crew, but she didn't mind.

She liked having the store to herself.

She could shop in peace, free to linger in the refrigerated section, comparing the prices of frozen dinners, or loiter in front of jars of pasta sauce, reading nutrition labels. At her leisure, she could wander and meander up and down the aisles.

Stopping near a large bin of packaged ruby red grapefruit, she checked the price.

$3.99 per bag.

Each bag contained five or six grapefruit, which worked out to roughly $0.66 to $0.80 cents per grapefruit. Not exactly a steal, despite the advertised special, but the purchase probably wouldn't put her over the $50.00 budget she allowed herself for the week.

And if it did, she could always leave the grapefruit.

Penny pinching, as her grandmother would call it, was annoying.

She hated trying to work out the prices to see if she could afford things, giving up one item at the expense of something else, having to choose between broccoli or spinach, unable to have both.

But it couldn't be helped.

Money wasn't exactly flowing into her bank account. Even though she had a job now, a long-term temporary assignment as an administrative assistant for an oilfield services company; the pay wasn't great, but it wasn't bad. She was making a bit more than she had at her last job, and the temp agency offered decent benefits.

Money hadn't been flowing since she'd given up "dating" three months ago.

She wouldn't pretend she didn't miss the perks of "dating." The money had been good, but the consequences and ramifications hadn't been worth it. As tempting as it was to "date" again, she couldn't bring herself to do it, wouldn't bring herself to take the risk, not after what happened with Ben Chang.

Even now, three months later, it was hard to believe she'd escaped the townhouse with her life. The next day, in the bathroom of Rae's small apartment, she'd stared at herself in the mirror, wondering why she hadn't been killed. By some divine intervention, or undeserved good fortune, she'd been spared, and she decided she would never put her life on the line again.

More than once or twice, she'd relived that night, forcing herself to remember the very moment when Ben had pulled the trigger. She still didn't know how he'd missed her and couldn't believe she'd jumped out of the way in time. By her own estimation, she should have gotten a bullet between the eyes, and yet, she was alive.

Pushing the disturbing thoughts away, Spencer steered the basket toward a bin of organic apples and frowned at the price, $5.99 a pound.

Organic fruit, another casualty of her decision to stop "dating."

Still, she didn't regret the decision, which annoyed Rae.

She'd told her sisters that the horrific experience in Ben's townhouse had convinced her to give up "dating" for good, but that wasn't entirely true.

Secretly, Spencer believed she'd reaped what she'd sown, suffering the consequences of sins she'd never wanted to commit. Guilt and self-condemnation had made her realize she could never "date" again.

Picking up a Golden Delicious apple, Spencer brought it to her nose, trying to detect a faint, sweet smell.

Eventually, time flew, and with no word from Ben and no cops banging on her door with questions about the money and watches she'd stolen, Spencer stopped having nightmares and looking over her shoulder.

The ordeal she'd lived through faded, leaving behind lingering memories of the two months she and Ben had spent getting to know one another. Somehow, she'd managed to dissociate Ben from the fact that he'd tried to kill her.

Sometimes, Spencer wondered if she might still be interested in Ben, even though that was impossible. There was no way she could have feelings for a man who'd pointed a gun in her face and pulled the trigger.

Still, she didn't think she could ever forget him.

Occasionally, a memory would encroach upon her mind, and overtake her thoughts before she realized it, and she would struggle to get rid of the memories before they took root and forced her down a lonely, twisted road of wild, hypothetical contemplation.

Spencer grabbed a bag of apples and put it in the basket.

The memories had to be stopped or she would end up entertaining ridiculous fantasies of seeing Ben again, picking up where they left off.

Before he pointed that gun in her face and pulled the trigger.

Before he ruined what chance, however slim, they might have had to—

"Hey, sweet girl ..."

Paralyzed, Spencer looked up, and her heart damn near stopped.

17

Houston, Texas
Randall's Grocery Store

Spencer had often thought of what she would do, or say, if she ever saw Ben again.

She'd constructed several scenarios where she was tough and badass and vengeful, taking no prisoners. But those were revenge fantasies, and she'd grown tired of indulging in them, wasting mental energy on something she was sure would never happen.

May, June, and July came and went with no contact from Ben, and Spencer resolved to forget him, to pretend he'd never existed, and whatever errant feelings remained in her heart, she'd ignored.

Spencer had figured she would never see Ben again.

But now, here he was, and she couldn't help but wonder if her wayward thoughts of him had conjured him up, made him manifest in the flesh.

Ben gave her the ironic smile she remembered too well. The curve of his mouth combined with the slight narrowing of his dark eyes always made her feel as if she had a secret, but he was the only one who knew it.

As Ben made his way toward her, her heart slammed, and she glanced around the produce area, searching for someone who could hear her scream, if it came to that, but there was no one, not even a stock boy.

Her emotions all over the place, she stared at him, frozen, not sure what to think, not sure what to do, as the memories she'd managed to bury came rushing toward her.

She was terrified and yet excited.

She didn't know what to think about Ben and didn't know how to wrap her mind around the fact that he was standing right in front of her. Where had he been? What did he want? Would he be cordial and friendly? Or was he about to go for her throat?

And how would she respond to him? How should she respond?

She didn't know whether she would push him away or pull him closer, but she hated herself for feeling both infatuated and indignant. She hated feeling so unsure, and she hated him for coming back into her life, tall and handsome, just like she remembered.

Nothing about him had changed, not even her confusing feelings for him, she realized.

Something was different, though, and it was probably insurmountable.

He'd tried to kill her.

Of course, she'd robbed him, and had probably deserved a bullet, but it didn't matter. Ben had tried to kill her, and because of that, it would be impossible to fall in love with him.

But falling in love wasn't on her list of things to do anyway, and never would be.

And maybe part of her was glad he'd tried to kill her, because the memory of the gun he'd pointed at her made it easy to convince herself she could never be with a man like him.

Unable to remember any of the grand soliloquies she'd composed in one of the many fantasies she'd created about encountering Ben again, Spencer decided her only option was to take the coward's way out.

Struggling to clear her throat, she looked up at him, and said, "I'm sorry. I think you have me confused with someone else ..."

"I figured you wouldn't be happy to see me." Ben laughed a bit. "But I didn't expect you would pretend you don't know me."

"I don't know you," she told him and realized it was true.

When she'd met Ben, he had claimed to be his own boss and told her he owned several check cashing and high-end cleaning services in a number of states, including Texas, and she'd believed him. She'd had no reason to dispute him, no reason to suspect he was anything more than a young, wealthy entrepreneur.

She didn't know what to think of him now.

Because the Ben she thought she knew, the man who'd sat next to her on that park bench in front of the reflecting pool, had been some carefully crafted persona.

A manufactured illusion of a kind, compassionate man who gave a damn about her.

The real Ben was a man who'd tried to put a bullet in her head.

And somehow, she had a feeling she wasn't the first person he'd shot at.

Ben was probably some kind of criminal, or involved in criminal activities.

Spencer thought of the guns she'd found in his closet and all the money, which had turned out to be over thirty thousand dollars, and the knives, and she felt stupid, like some dumb, gullible girl, easily fooled.

The weapons and the cash had bothered her, and yet she'd decided to dismiss those worrisome feelings.

But why had she ignored her intuition?

Because Ben was handsome and rich, and she had been tired of "dating?"

For a moment, after she'd met Ben, Spencer had indulged in the idea of wanting someone to take care of her. "Dating" paid the bills, but just barely. There never seemed enough money for extra indulgences. No matter what she collected and gave to Rae to fence, it seemed her sister never got what Spencer thought the items were worth.

"Dating" was supposed to have given her financial freedom, but she still felt like she was scratching and scrounging for crumbs, something she'd had to do her whole life. She wanted security and wanted someone else to bear her burdens, to rush in and rescue her, financially, not romantically.

That idea had been a moment of weakness, she realized now.

Relying on men had failed her mother, time after time, and Spencer had decided she would never depend on a man; she would rely on herself, make it on her own.

But then she'd met Ben, and she made the mistake of thinking she didn't have to be so tough and badass and self-reliant.

Stupid, she knew.

Spencer took a few steps backward, turned the basket in a 180-degree arc, and pushed it forward, her pulse racing as she headed toward a bin of bananas.

Seconds later, firm fingers wrapped around the back of her arm, and she jumped, even though she wasn't surprised.

"You really going to pretend you don't know me."

She wanted to, but pretense was an exercise in futility and exhaustion, and her nerves were shot; she didn't think she could keep it together enough to fool Ben.

Spencer sighed and then faced him. "What do you want?"

"I want you …" he said, smiling a little, "to help me out with something…"

"Help you out?" she asked, disappointed that her heart had started to pound when he'd said he wanted her, and she was ashamed at her hopes for rising.

"I need you to do me a favor."

"I already did you a favor," she snapped, sneaking a glance around the produce section again, wondering where the cameras were, and hoping the store surveillance would keep Ben from trying to hurt her. "I didn't go to the police and tell them that you tried to kill me."

Ben stared at her. "I didn't try to kill you, sweet girl."

"Oh, really? You didn't?" she scoffed, glaring at him. "Then what do you call pointing a gun in my face and pulling the trigger? If that's not trying to kill me, then—"

"I wasn't pointing that gun at you, sweet girl."

"You think I'm crazy?" she asked. "You think I don't know whether or not I was staring down the barrel of that gun?"

Ben reached into her basket and picked up the bag of grapefruit. "It hurts me that you think I would shoot you, sweet girl."

She stared at him, determined not to be taken in by his "sweet girl" endearment.

"I wasn't trying to kill you," Ben said. "I was aiming at the man standing behind you."

"The man standing behind me?" She shook her head. "There was no man standing behind me. There was only you standing in front of me and pointing that damn gun at me."

He put the bag of grapefruit back in the basket and then looked at her. "I would never hurt you, sweet girl. I'm telling you the truth. That night, a man broke into my house. I'm surprised you didn't see him. Little Chinese bastard, had a green snake tattooed across his face."

"A man with a snake tattooed on his face?" She gave him a short, bitter laugh. "Wow, Ben, you must really think I'm stupid."

"I think you're a lot of things, sweet girl," he said. "But stupid is not one of them."

She glanced at him, wary of his sly smile.

"You know, sweet girl, I would like to think that you didn't tell the cops I tried to kill you because you know in your heart that I didn't," Ben said, folding his arms and looking at her like he'd already figured her out and was just waiting for her to catch a clue. "But, the truth is, I suspect, that you didn't go to the cops because you were looking out for yourself."

Spencer said, "I didn't say anything because I was afraid you would try to kill me again."

Ben shook his head and smiled a little. "No, sweet girl, you didn't say anything because you didn't want to tell the cops what you were doing in my house."

Apprehensive, she said, "I was at your house at your invitation."

"An invitation you accepted so you could steal from me," Ben said, his dark eyes cold despite the smile. "You took advantage of my hospitality."

"What are you talking about?" Spencer stared at him, blood rushing through her ears. "I didn't steal anything from you."

"You're not a good liar, sweet girl." Ben told her. "But you look so pretty trying to pretend you didn't go into my closet and steal my money and my Rolex watches."

"I don't know what the hell you're talking about …" She tried to push the lies from her dry mouth. "I didn't steal anything from you."

Ben stared at her. "You stole more than you think."

She looked away, not sure what he meant, not sure she really wanted to know.

Exhaling, he said, "What else do you need besides grapefruit?"

Perplexed by, and yet grateful for, his abrupt change of subject, Spencer pulled a small yellow Post-It note from the back pocket of her jeans and held it out to him.

After reading it, Ben slipped an arm through hers and smiled.

"Come on, sweet girl," he said. "Let's finish up your shopping."

18

Houston, Texas
Randall's Grocery Store

Ben dropped several packages of pasta into the basket, overloaded with all the things on Spencer's list plus dozens of other items, extra things she probably couldn't afford.

"So, what did you spend the money on, sweet girl?"

Spencer tensed, hesitating; she still wanted to pretend she didn't know what money he was talking about, wanted to deny the truth.

But Ben's dark eyes and mysterious smile reminded her of the mistakes she'd made, churning up the shame and guilt she'd managed to suppress.

Shaking her head, Spencer said, "I didn't spend it ..."

"Why not?"

Spencer shrugged, turning the basket down the baking goods aisle.

She didn't want to tell him she'd been too afraid to spend it; the money was connected to the terror she suffered, and she'd thought if she spent it, more bad things would happen. She'd believed the money was cursed, feared it would bring her nothing but bad luck.

"You still have the money?"

"Not anymore …" She stopped the basket near several rows of cake mixes.

"I don't understand," he said. "You didn't spend it, but you don't have it?"

Spencer walked to the boxes of Duncan Hines. "I gave it away …"

"You gave my money away?"

Grabbing a box of spice cake, Spencer faced Ben. "I made an anonymous donation to a homeless shelter."

"A homeless shelter?"

"Despite what you think"—She tossed the cake mix in the basket and then walked to him—"I'm not entirely selfish and heartless."

"I never thought you were selfish and heartless," he said. "Even though you left me to die."

She winced. "I didn't leave you to die."

"You put a knife in my gut," he reminded her. "And then you ran away as I called to you for help."

"I didn't know what the hell was going on, or what was happening," she said and then stepped closer to him, lowering her voice. "I thought you already knew I had stolen from you and you were trying to kill me because of it. I didn't know you were aiming at some burglar."

"I would never hurt you, sweet girl."

"I find that hard to believe." She slipped her arm through his again as they continued down the aisle. "I'll bet you hate me and want me dead."

"Why would I hate you?"

She glanced at the shelves stocked with bags of sugar and then back at him. "Because I stole from you."

"I can't throw stones, sweet girl," he said. "I think you were doing what you thought you had to do to survive."

Spencer steered the basket down the next aisle, looking for coffee, drawn by the rich aroma.

He was right about her doing what she'd had to in order to survive.

But her survival instincts hadn't kicked in because she had some bill that was past due or because she was struggling to put food on the table.

She'd "dated" Ben because she'd had to survive the onslaught of crazy emotions, making her think it was okay to fall in love with him.

And nothing could be further from the truth.

She wouldn't survive giving her heart to him.

No one escaped love unscathed.

"I understand that desperate fight for survival."

"I find that hard to believe," she quipped, giving him the side eye.

"But I do," he said. "I had to survive being stabbed by a beautiful woman that I cared about, and still do care about, a woman I thought cared about me."

"I'm sorry I stabbed you," she rushed out, barely able to meet his gaze. "And I'm glad you're okay."

"You didn't hit any major organs or arteries," he said.

"So, what happened after I left?" she ventured to ask, still bothered by the memory of her hasty reaction. "Did you call 9-1-1, or ..."

"There was no need to call the cops," Ben told her, looking toward bottles of flavored coffee syrup. "I took care of the intruder."

"What does that mean?" Spencer asked, not sure she really wanted to know. "How did you take care of him?"

"I made sure he understood that it was a mistake to break into my house and try to take what belongs to me," Ben said, turning to stare at her. "There are consequences when you make mistakes."

Spencer looked down, well aware of the message he'd given her, the subtle threat.

Just like the intruder with the snake tattoo on his face, she would have to suffer for her stupid mistake.

She just prayed those consequences wouldn't be too severe and that she would be able to withstand whatever punishment Ben had planned for her.

He probably did still like her, but his feelings wouldn't stop him from making her pay.

What was it called? Tough love. No, not love. What they shared wasn't anything close to love. But she had a feeling their situation wasn't very far away, either. She didn't know how to define it, and maybe a definition wasn't necessary right now.

"You and I are not so different," Ben said as they headed toward small bags of pre-packaged coffee beans. "We both have made tough choices, and some people would call those choices mistakes."

"Some people would call those choices crimes," Spencer pointed out, grabbing a large can of Columbian coffee from the bottom shelf.

"The favor you're going to do for me won't be anything criminal." Ben took the coffee and then found a place for it in the basket.

"Who the hell says I'm going to be doing you a favor?" She looked up at him, feeling strangely sassy and domesticated, almost like a wife, and yet wary.

"Maybe *favor* is not the best word, because it makes you think you have a choice in the matter," Ben said. "The truth is, you owe me, sweet girl, and I don't want you to find out what happens to people who don't pay their debts."

19

Spencer didn't think she would ever make love with Ben again.

And yet, they'd already made love three times tonight.

How the hell had this happened?

One minute, they were walking out of the grocery store and heading to her small, used hatchback where he'd loaded the grocery bags in the back seat.

And the next, she was following him to his place, at his request.

Despite all the warnings screaming in her head, Spencer found herself at his house.

In the three months since she'd seen him, he had apparently moved from the townhouse in mid-town and settled himself in a new place, an expansive, two-story Colonial in the gated Players' Woods community in The Woodlands, north of Houston.

It was a beautiful home with spacious rooms and high-end finishes and upgrades, marble and granite and exotic hardwoods.

As soon as Ben led her through the double-door entrance and

into the large foyer, she imagined what it would be like if it was their house, because they were together, because maybe she was his wife …

With strange fantasies in her head, it wasn't hard to convince herself to let him take her up the curving stairway and into his bedroom.

Conflicted, Spencer closed her eyes and listened to his heart beating.

There was something compelling, and magnetic, about Ben Chang.

When she was with him, she wasn't sure who she was.

Ben made her forget about the foundation she'd built herself upon, the self-reliance and mistrust that had served her well and protected her from disappointment.

With Ben, she always felt too close to abandoning her reluctance to love and romance, and yet, she didn't know if she wanted to be with him.

She didn't know if she wanted to be without him either.

Earlier at the grocery store when it was time to check out, the total had been over three hundred dollars, and before she could recover from the shock, before she could begin the embarrassing process of removing some of the items, Ben stepped in and paid for everything.

Spencer had made a half-hearted, feeble attempt to protest, but when he pulled out the black AmEx card, she felt a traitorous rush of thrilling adrenaline; the self-reliance and self-sufficiency was ignored, and all she wanted was to be taken care of …

"Sweet girl, I heard a story about a woman who tried to scam a man," Ben said, breaking the silence they'd settled into after their last round of vigorous sex. "She put something in his drink."

Cuddling next to him, Spencer listened and tried not to worry.

"When the man passed out, the woman robbed him," he said,

his voice deep, the Island lilt hypnotic, almost like a lullaby. "She took his money, his Cartier watch, all his valuables, his car."

Tensing in his arms, she grew anxious, apprehensive.

"He didn't remember what had happened to him for a few days." Ben pulled her closer. "But soon, it started coming back to him, and finally, he got his memory back, and he realized what the woman had done, and do you know what he did?"

Spencer held her breath, afraid of what would happen when Ben got to the end of his grim tale.

"He didn't do anything," Ben said, trailing his fingers down her spine. "He chalked it up to a lesson learned, don't trust a beautiful girl, or something like that."

Spencer waited, sensing there was more to the story.

"I thought if something like that ever happened to me, I would go after this deceptive woman, and I would hurt her very badly, the police would find her body, beaten beyond recognition."

Her pulse jumped, and she tried to push away from him, but he held her tighter, his strong, muscled arms like chains imprisoning her.

"I might even kill this treacherous woman," Ben said, "if I didn't need her help with something very important to me."

Disquieted, she swallowed the hot mass in her throat. "So, what are you saying?"

"I told you," he said. "I need a favor, and you need to pay your debt."

"What kind of favor?" she asked, her heart starting to punch, as she tried to figure out what the favor might be, afraid of what Ben was really involved in and that it would be dangerous. Would she have to risk her life as a favor to Ben just for being stupid enough to steal from him? Would she have to commit a crime?

"One you might enjoy. I want you to go to Belize on vacation and stay at a beautiful resort called the Belizean Banyan. Once you are there, I will let you know what to do next."

Street lamps outside the ceiling-to-floor windows allowed a jaundiced, diffused glow into the bedroom casting strange, eerie shadows, like the macabre, grotesque shapes that used to creep across the walls and torment her as a child.

"And what if I don't pay my debt?" she ventured, suspicious, knowing that Ben wanted her to do more than just enjoy a vacation in Belize. "Are you going to kill me?"

"Don't make me be the bad guy, okay." He took her hand and brought it to his lips. "Don't force me to threaten you."

"How could I force you to threaten me?"

"You put me in a position I never wanted to be in when you stole from me," he told her. "You made me question everything I thought about you, and now I don't know if I can trust you."

"You can't trust me? Are you serious?" Angry, she pushed away from him, moving to the opposite side of the bed. Sitting up, she reached toward the lamp on the bed table, and turned it on. "What about everything I thought about you?"

"What did you think about me?" he asked. "Did you think I would be easy to steal from? Did you think you're so beautiful, I would let you get away with it?"

"I didn't think you were the kind of person who would try to kill me," she snapped.

"I wasn't trying to kill you," he said. "I told you, someone broke into my house, and—"

"The man with the green snake on his face," she said, rolling her eyes. "Yeah, that's what you said, but I didn't see anybody—"

"I'm telling you the truth," he said. "That man broke into my house, and you should know, sweet girl, that if he had killed me, he would have done much worse to you, and I wasn't going to let that happen. I had to protect you."

"I didn't ask you to protect me!" she said. "I didn't ask you to do anything for me!"

"You should have asked," Ben said. "Instead of just taking what you wanted because you didn't trust me to give it to you."

"You wouldn't have given me anything." She shook her head, pulling the smooth, cool bed sheets up toward her neck. "Nobody has ever given me anything. I've always had to fight for everything, and even when I fight, I never win ..."

"You didn't fight for us," he said. "If you had, you would have won. I would have made sure of it."

She looked at him. "You think there was an us?"

Ben nodded, sitting up. "There still could be."

"But only if I help you out," she said. "There's not going to be an 'us' unless I do this favor for you, right?"

"There's not going to be an 'us' unless I can trust you." He adjusted the pillows behind him and then leaned back.

"So, this favor you want me to do." Warning herself not to cry and trying to keep her voice calm, she went on, "It's some kind of test? And if I pass, then we get to be together?"

"I'm not trying to test you, sweet girl." He reached for her, pulling her back toward him. "I think we'd both be disappointed in the results."

Spencer looked away, not sure what to think; she didn't know what he was asking of her and didn't know what he really wanted from their relationship, or whatever it was they were engaging and indulging in together.

She was equally confused about what, if anything, she wanted from him.

Protection from all those annoying disappointments life had always offered her? Financial security? Good sex? No, great sex. Companionship? Fellowship? Love? No, not love.

Damn it!

What the hell was wrong with her?

She hardly recognized this strange version of herself, a woman willing to risk her sanity and dignity for a chance to fall in love with a man who'd threatened her.

What kind of crazy, desperate bitch had she turned into?

"I want to have you in my life, sweet girl." He kissed her forehead, gathering her in his arms. "But not if you are going to steal from me or force me to be a bad guy."

"What does that mean, force you to be the bad guy?" She moved her head to look up at him. "Are you going to hurt me because I took your money? That story you told me about the girl who tried to scam a guy wasn't really some story you heard, was it? You know that's how I get into men's closets, don't you? And you said you would kill the treacherous bitch if she stole from you, and I stole from you, so ..."

"If I really thought you were a treacherous bitch, sweet girl," he said, stroking her cheek, "you would be dead right now, I promise you."

The sincerity of his unveiled admission caught her off guard and sent her blood pressure soaring, but it sparked a hint of rage, too. Struggling to summon the defiance lying dormant within her, she said, "And how do you know I'm not treacherous?"

"Because you're still alive."

Her rage intensified a bit, and she pushed away again.

But Ben pulled her back. "I'm not trying to be the bad guy, sweet girl."

"You could have fooled me," she said, no longer content and complacent in his arms. "What do you call forcing me to help you with some favor?"

Smiling, he said, "The consequence of your mistake."

———

Note from Rachel

Thanks so much for taking the time to read Flawless Mistake. I hope you enjoyed it as much as I enjoyed writing it.

Honest reviews by readers are the most powerful way to help others discover my books. Please consider taking one minute to share your thoughts on the book by rating and reviewing it. I'd be eternally grateful!

Click here to post a review!

https://www.amazon.com/review/create-review?
asin=B013Z9YO2M

FLAWLESS DANGER

SNEAK PREVIEW

Are you ready to read the next book in The Spencer & Sione Series? Check out the sneak preview of Flawless Danger — the first 13 chapters for you to try before you buy!

Just turn or swipe the page and keep reading ...

1

**The Woodlands, Texas
Players' Woods Community**

Thin ice skimmed along the surface of her skin.

Lids fluttering, Spencer Edwards opened her eyes and then immediately closed them, regretting her decision to escape the unrestrained darkness of unconsciousness.

She preferred the black void of dreams she would never remember.

But the cold line trailing across her cheek was too confusing to ignore.

She opened her eyes again. Sun streamed into the room from three large rectangular ceiling-to-floor windows across from the king-sized bed.

Annoyed by the harsh morning rays, she turned her head from the windows. Spencer frowned, her heart kicking as she stared at the sun reflected on the gleaming blade of the knife hovering inches from her face.

"Good morning, sweet girl," Ben Chang said. Lying next to

her, propped up on his left elbow, he held the knife with his right hand. "How did you sleep?"

Spencer couldn't answer him, couldn't take her eyes off the razor-sharp blade. He held the knife casually, almost carelessly, as though it was some benign trinket, as though he couldn't use it to slice her throat open, or slash her face to ribbons.

"Do you recognize this knife, sweet girl?" Ben asked.

Hardly able to breathe, Spencer followed the blade as it inched closer to her face and then descended beyond her line of sight.

Her heart slammed.

Cold steel skimmed the curve of her jaw.

Panic, terror, and confusion converged upon her, leaving her unable to speak or move, incapable of any coherent, logical thought.

Trailing the flat part of the blade across her cheek, Ben said, "You should remember this knife very well." The thin spine of the knife glided over her neck and down over her collarbone.

Trembling, she stared at Ben, her blood colder than the knife trailing along her shoulder.

Was he going to kill her? Would she die a horrific, bloody death? Would he stab her over and over until the sheets were soaked with her blood?

"This is the knife you stabbed me with, sweet girl."

A moment later, Spencer felt cold steel against her breasts. The scream she should have put into the atmosphere was strangled, silenced by terror and lust. Ben lifted the blade from her skin. Swinging his arm overhead in a swift arc, he stabbed the knife into the tufted leather headboard and moved on top of her.

Knowing what he wanted, Spencer didn't deny him. She wanted the same thing, even though she knew, when it was over, she would hate herself for giving into him, for being so desperate and shameless.

She stared at the mural on the tray ceiling. It was different from the one on the ceiling in the townhouse bedroom, but still just as violent and bloody.

A dragon and a tiger fighting to the death.

Unlike the mural in the townhouse, this painting had words on the first panel.

The tiger will strike with claws.

The dragon will consume with fire.

In one section of the vivid, lurid drawing, the dragon used his tail as a weapon, thrusting the razor-sharp spines into the tiger's powerful flank.

Gazing at another section of the mural, she gasped and clutched his shoulders as the sensations began to overwhelm her. Though wounded, the tiger sank a claw into the dragon's back, between the scales, piercing the delicate flesh beneath the armor.

The sensations began to rocket through her, becoming almost overpowering as something violent and primitive took hold of her. Wrapping her arms around Ben's neck, Spencer struggled to catch her breath as the feelings became overbearing.

Ben was rough with her, but she didn't want tender caresses. She didn't want gentle lovemaking to fool her or trick her into thinking he gave a damn about her.

Her eyes roamed across the mural to a section where the dragon swung his tail and penetrated the tiger's side with the tip, pushing his tail deep into the tiger until the tiger was impaled upon him.

Something barbaric broke within her, and Spencer succumbed to an explosion of desperate thrashing. As the tumult subsided and her heart began to slow, she went limp.

Tracing his fingers along her cheek, Ben kissed her and lifted his head, smiling at her.

"Sonofabitch!" Spencer screamed and slapped him.

He cursed, shock in his dark gaze.

Flipping on her stomach, Spencer belly-crawled across the

damp, crumpled sheets and flopped over the side of the bed to the floor.

No sooner had she hit the stamped carpet than she was on her feet, sprinting across the room to the chair were she'd flung her clothes after hastily discarding them last night. Stumbling, she grabbed her shirt, pulled it over her head, then slipped into her jeans, and ran to the bedroom door.

Grabbing the knob, she opened it and—

A whispery swish, near her ear, too close, and then a thud against the doorframe.

Spencer turned her head to the left.

Her heart jumped and then dropped, as she saw the reflection of her own wild, wide-eyed stare in the blade jutting from the wood where the tip of the knife had penetrated the frame. Her fear exploding into rage, Spencer grabbed the hilt of the knife and yanked. The tip of the blade remained in the doorframe. Screaming, she struggled to pull it free, determined to pull the knife out.

Determined to kill Ben before he could kill her.

Spurred by visions of sinking the blade into him again, Spencer gritted her teeth, clutched the hilt with both hands, and yanked. The knife dislodged. Stumbling back, Spencer turned. Ben was almost right on her, moments away.

Undaunted, Spencer raised the knife, but he overshadowed her, smothering her with a powerful arm that snaked around her and dragged her toward him. Trapped in his hostile embrace, she wrestled against him, desperate and disoriented, not sure where she began and he ended or where she ended and he began.

She wasn't even sure where the knife was until he grabbed her wrist, tightening his fingers like a vise.

"Not again, sweet girl," Ben said, glaring down at her. "You will never get another chance to put this knife in my gut again. You will never get another chance to leave me bleeding on the floor, begging for your help, watching as you turn and walk away from me, leaving me to die." He jerked her toward him, twisting her wrist.

Crying out, Spencer's death grip on the hilt slipped, and the knife fell from her hand as Ben held her closer, tighter, crushing her against him.

2

_____

The Woodlands, Texas
Players' Woods Community

"You know, sweet girl, there is something I have been wondering," Ben said.

Arms crossed, disgruntled and hostile, Spencer sat on a wicker stool at the island in Ben's bright, yellow and French country blue kitchen. As the sun streamed in, warm and ethereal, she struggled to reconcile the feelings of domesticity with the rage racing through her blood. The cozy surroundings were disconcerting, and she fought to remember who Ben Chang really was—a devious asshole and not the kind, caring man he'd tricked her into thinking he was, the man she wanted him to be.

Standing at the gas range, Ben was making her an omelet. As she stared at the muscles beneath his smooth, deep chocolate skin, she felt her body responding. He didn't have a shirt on, and the boxer briefs he wore left little to the imagination, reminding her of their tumultuous lovemaking. Spencer looked away, disgusted with herself, wishing she'd never me him on that beautiful afternoon.

Sitting on a park bench in front of the Houston City Hall reflecting pool, Spencer couldn't help but think that the weather was too lovely for her to be so depressed. But how could she not be desolate after the disastrous interview she'd suffered through earlier that morning? She'd missed her chance for honest, gainful employment. So unless she wanted to starve, have her car repossessed, and get evicted from her apartment, she'd have to continue "dating" old men—drugging them and stealing from them.

Spencer had been close to tears when, peripherally, she became aware of someone sitting next to her. Annoyed, she'd rolled her eyes. Why the hell had someone decided to sit next to her? Most of the benches lined around the perimeter of the park were empty. Why couldn't she be left alone to enjoy the grand, lavish pity party she'd thrown for herself? Wasn't it a party she deserved, having just blown her interview at a leading oil and gas conglomerate?

Irritated by the interruption of her lamentations, Spencer was about to move to another bench when a deep, enchanting, lyrical baritone said, "You okay?"

The stranger's concern seemed genuine, and as their conversation continued, she found herself intrigued by his island accent. Her interest increased as his compassion intensified, and when he asked her out to dinner, she didn't turn him down.

She should have told him to go to hell. Instead, she'd spent two months getting to know Benjamin Chang.

But the tilt-a-whirl romance started to scare Spencer. She worried she might be falling in love, something she'd promised herself she would never do. Allowing carefree romance to turn into love wasn't going to happen, not ever, not for her. But her aversion to love wasn't the result of some tortuous heartbreak, or any rampant issues of low self-worth.

Spencer had her mother to blame. She supposed her mother could be blamed for most of the problems she'd suffered throughout her life. And most of those problems had started the day her mother had walked out of their small, hot apartment, leaving Spencer to fend for herself.

Child abandonment. Spencer hated the word *abandonment* and what it had meant in her life. Abandonment was frightening and embarrassing, but it had happened to her. She'd been abandoned —a neglected, discarded seven-year-old with purple bruises covering her arms and legs like tattoos. If not for the love and support of her grandmother, she would have ended up in foster care, a potentially worse predicament. But, the abandonment hadn't been forever.

The prodigal mother came back five years later, when Spencer was twelve. Claiming to be a changed woman, the former absentee mother promised that she was different and wanted the chance to be the mother Spencer deserved. She'd found God and herself her mother had told the judge, and he'd been convinced. Though, it was more likely her mother's beauty, and not her convictions, that had swayed him.

And her mother had been different. Gone was the woman who could be hyper and obsessive one moment and then violent and enraged the next. There was no more screaming and cursing. Her mother no longer threw things and broke dishes as she ranted and raged.

And the physical abuse was nonexistent.

No more slaps and kicks.

No having a pillow pressed against her face as she struggled desperately to breathe.

The violent mother was gone, but in her place was someone even worse. A needy, pathetic woman who had been more than willing to degrade herself in order to keep her husband, the first of three, it would turn out to be. Mommy dearest's three doomed marriages had terrorized Spencer, leaving her with a palpable disdain and distrust of holy matrimony.

Love sent a woman to the depths of despair. Marriage was

even worse, as it turned a woman into what Spencer thought of as "that wife"—a clinging woman who would humiliate and demean herself to please her man.

Sighing, Spencer stared at the glass of grapefruit juice Ben had poured her, fortified with a healthy dose of vodka. To calm her nerves, he'd claimed. As if liquor could erase the terror and trauma of waking up to a knife in her face that could have ended up in her back instead of the doorframe.

"How did you get into this business of drugging men and stealing from them?" Ben asked.

Spencer said nothing.

"You're a beautiful woman," Ben said. "Why would you risk stealing expensive things from men who would probably fall all over themselves to give them to you if you just asked?"

"I would have to do more than ask." She stared at the vodka-laden grapefruit juice, tempted to grab it.

"That's true," he said and then poured a bit too much vodka into his own glass of grapefruit juice. "You'd probably also have to smile."

Again, Spencer stayed quiet.

"Are you one of those women who gets turned on by the idea of getting caught taking something that doesn't belong to her?"

"I'm one of those women who has bills to pay," she said. "I'm one of those women who lost her job and then couldn't find another one, and then ..."

"And then what?"

"It doesn't matter," she said. "You wouldn't understand and neither would you care."

"I care more than you think, sweet girl," he said. "Maybe more than I should."

Rolling her eyes, Spencer glanced out the window over the sink, refusing to believe he'd ever cared about her, or even had the ability to give a damn. "Why don't you tell me something," she said. "How did you find out about me? Who told you that I—"

"That you drug old men and rob them blind?"

Deaf, dumb, and blind, she thought, remembering what Rae always said.

"Well, it is a sad, but interesting, tale of betrayal and heart-break." Ben slid the omelet from the skillet onto a plate, then turned, and reached across the island to sit the plate in front of her. "It's the story of a young handsome industrious and enter-prising entrepreneur who made the mistake of extending his compassion, concern, and caring to a beautiful woman who he thought was sweet and kind, but who turned out to be devious and treacherous."

"Are you going to answer me anytime soon?" she asked, not in the mood to be shamed by his ridiculous theatrics.

"The devious woman stabbed the compassionate entrepreneur, in an act of cold-blooded mercilessness, and left him to die, even though he begged and pleaded with her for help," Ben said. "Somehow, he was able to crawl to a phone and call nine-one-one. A few weeks later, the man went away to recuperate."

Spencer rolled her eyes.

"During his sabbatical, the man was visited by a very good friend, whom he confided in about his disappointment. The man's friend was livid at the woman's callous treatment of the man, and he set out to find out why the woman had done the man wrong. The friend decided to look into the woman's background—"

"Look into my background?" She stared at him, her heart racing. "You had somebody investigate me?"

"The friend learned several interesting things about the woman," Ben said, disregarding her questions. "And he shared his findings with the man. It turned out that the woman had a treacherous half-sister, a woman named Desarae Bedard."

Spencer looked away, her heart racing with fear now, the rage eclipsed by panic and confusion.

"Desarae Bedard, the man's friend learned, was the star of her own sick, twisted plot," Ben said and then smiled. "Two years ago, Desarae Bedard had been accused of murdering a wealthy investment banker and his wife. She was cleared, but the subsequent criminal investigation revealed that she had been the investment banker's secret mistress."

Spencer scowled at him, not surprised that he'd belittled Rae's terror and heartbreak, reducing her sister's anguish to the most sordid details.

"Following the investment banker's death, she became involved with a man named Mr. Cephas, a disbarred lawyer who reinvented himself as a high-class fence," Ben said. "The man's friend informed him that Mr. Cephas often fenced expensive items for Desarae Bedard, who stole them from the rich men she went to dinner with and then drugged. Now, Mr. Cephas, in an act of hospitality, was rumored to have also extended his fencing expertise to Desarae Bedard's younger sister, Spencer Edwards, the treacherous woman who stabbed the compassionate entrepreneur."

"Who is this *friend* you told to check me out?" Spencer demanded. "How did he find out that stuff about me and Rae? Who told him?"

"I have no idea who told him," Ben said. "I only wish he hadn't told me. Finding out more about you made me understand your actions even less."

She dropped her gaze to the omelet, the shame returning. Ben's confusion mirrored hers. When she'd made the decision to "date" Ben, her reasons had made perfect sense. Now, she realized that what she'd thought was logical was actually lunacy.

"I guess I don't understand how you had the guts to do it," Ben said, bracing his hands against the edge of the island as he glared at her. "You weren't scared of getting caught?"

Spencer considered his question, a query she wasn't sure how to answer. When Ben had fallen asleep, she hadn't been content about the idea of stealing from him. Convinced that "dating" him was her only option, she'd let misguided convictions lead her into the closet, where she'd found the Rolex watches and cash. Once the loot was in her Coach bag, her only concern was getting out of the house.

And she did get out. Eventually. But not before she'd encountered Ben holding a large gun and pointing it right in her face.

"I guess, sweet girl, I wonder, why me?" Ben asked. "How did you choose me as a target? You usually go for more mature gentlemen."

Spencer didn't know what to say. She hadn't wanted to steal from Ben, but she felt she had no choice. At the time, she'd thought she was falling for him, and the easiest way to stop her descent into romantic madness was to never see Ben again. But she needed a good reason to walk away from him.

Her older sister's "Dating Protocol" had given her the reason. According to Rae's rules, you could only "date" a man once. After "dating" a guy, you weren't supposed to have anything to do with him, just in case the GHB hadn't been completely effective.

Spencer had reasoned that if she "dated" Ben, she couldn't see him again. If she never saw him again, then she couldn't fall in love with him. If she didn't fall in love with him, then she wouldn't become "that wife." Slippery slope logic, she realized now.

"You know, sweet girl," Ben said and then folded his arms. "I just realized that when I was recounting the compassionate entrepreneur's sad tale of woe, I completely left out the most important part."

"And what part was that?"

"I didn't tell you why I went away to recuperate," Ben said, then walked around the island, and stood beside her. "You remember I told you about the man who broke into my home that night?"

"The man with the green snake tattoo on his face?" She glanced up, giving him the side-eye.

Resting an arm on the back of her chair, Ben lowered his head until his mouth was inches from her ear. "I wanted to find out how the hell that man got into my home," he said. "And so I decided to take a look and see."

Puzzled, she turned her head a fraction and found his mouth merely a breath away. Ignoring the warm skittering feeling below her navel, she said, "Take a look and see what?"

"Come with me," he said, whispering the words against her skin. "I'll show you."

Moments later, in the spacious living room, Ben picked up a remote control from a side table and then told Spencer to take a seat. Wary, she perched on the edge of the black, oversized leather couch, her hands clasped between her knees.

"This is the video from my interior surveillance cameras," Ben said.

Her heart dropped as she stared at him. "Interior surveillance cameras?"

"I had them in every room of the townhouse," he said, facing the seventy-inch television against the wall as he pointed the remote control at the screen.

"In every room?"

"Yes, sweet girl," he said and then turned his head to give her a smile. "There was even a camera in the closet."

A moment later, the screen flickered and then came to life.

"What we are going to view is raw footage," he said. "The video feed from the interior surveillance camera in my closet which I copied onto a DVD."

Sick at the stomach, Spencer grabbed the edge of the couch seat, trying to brace herself. Nothing could have prepared her for the black-and-white images on the screen in front of her. Rigid, nails digging into the leather, she watched herself in the video, trying to deal with the disconnected feeling of seeing herself doing things she still couldn't believe she'd done; the woman on screen, removing the watches and money, seemed like someone else, and yet it was her.

"So, that's how you knew I stole from you."

"That's how I knew."

"Now what? You going to show that video to the cops? You gonna have me arrested?"

"I thought about it," Ben said. "It's what you deserve. Five to ten behind bars. But then I thought, maybe I can use this video for good and not evil. Maybe I can use it to teach you a lesson, one that you won't forget. Maybe I can use this video to make you suffer, the way I suffered that night after you stabbed me and left me to die. Maybe you need to see how it feels to wonder if your next breath will be your last ... I managed to call nine-one-one, and then I passed out. Woke up in a hospital. I don't know how many days had passed. I hardly knew who the hell I was. Took me several days to remember what had happened to me. And then, one day, the memories came rushing in like a flood, damn near drowning me. And then, I couldn't get what you had done to me out of my head, even though I wanted to. I wanted to forget. I even wanted to forgive. But I couldn't. There were days when it was almost like I could feel that knife plunging into my gut. I told myself I had to find you. I couldn't let you get away with what you'd done. And that is why, sweet girl, you owe me this favor."

Trembling, she stared up at him. "What is this damn favor about?"

"I told you last night." He sat on the coffee table, facing her. "I want you to go to Belize, and once you are there, I will let you know what to do next."

3

Belize City, Belize
Goldson International Airport

Spencer ducked her head as she climbed into the taxi and slid across the stained, careworn bench seat, announcing her destination to the man behind the wheel. "Belizean Banyan Resort."

Nodding, the driver shifted gears and pulled away from the curb, leaving the airport.

It was a lovely day, with an expansive blue sky, brilliant white clouds, and a shimmering sun. Spencer hardly noticed. She was unable to concentrate on the lush, tropical scenery. Collapsing against the seat, she took a deep breath, and tried to calm down.

The two-hour flight from Houston had been hell. Despite four glasses of wine, she hadn't been able to relax. Every other minute, panic had assailed her, flooding her mind with thoughts of the night she and Ben had made love for the very first time. The night she'd made a mistake so horrible, it was almost perfect.

An absolutely flawless mistake that had taken her to hell and back. Except she wasn't back—not yet. She wouldn't be back until she completed the favor for Ben.

The cab turned from the main highway and onto a side road cut through what seemed to be a small village of clapboard houses. Spencer stared out the window at the yards littered with junked cars, dilapidated furniture, and clothes swinging in the breeze on thin lines stretched between trees.

As the cab driver followed the curving road, Spencer couldn't stop worrying, wondering what Ben wanted her to do. He'd said it would be a favor, but it hadn't taken him long to let her know that he wasn't really asking for her help.

You owe me, sweet girl.

She'd stolen from him. Now she had a debt to pay.

Consequences for your mistakes.

Spencer stared out at the countryside, taking in the wide fields of grass dotted with bunches of low bushes and vibrant wild-flowers.

Farther inland, scrub brush clung to the ground, spreading in and around various shrubs and saplings. Beyond the trees, clumps of vegetation climbed up the slope of a verdant mountain that loomed toward the sky.

She'd never been to the small Central American country before but had heard others rave about the beauty of its coral reefs and jungles and its cultural significance as the site of various Mayan ruins.

Looking away from the lush scenery, Spencer crossed her arms, feeling both defiant and forlorn. Her fellow travelers had been an eclectic mix of nationalities and socio-economic types, all of them excited about their Belizean adventure, reading guide-books and discussing plans for excursions.

But there would be no zip-lining through the jungle for her.

Spencer's next move was to check into the Belizean Banyan Resort in San Ignacio, part of *Step One*, Ben had explained. The favor was comprised of several steps. After she completed a step, Ben would tell her the next step. This pattern would continue until the last step, which would be the satisfaction of the debt she owed.

An hour or so later, the driver turned into the town of San Ignacio. As he navigated the narrow, dusty streets, they passed various stores and businesses, most of them in states of disrepair, giving the place a sheen of squalor that Spencer found both deplorable and charming.

Along the crumbling, concrete road, listless dogs meandered aimlessly, while locals loitered in the doorways of restaurants and bars that had seen better days.

After coming much too close to a group of backpacking tourists hiking down the shoulder, the driver turned the cab onto a side road and sped along the ribbon of gravel cut through large trees with broad leaves.

The road ended, and the resort came into view.

Beyond a large clearing of manicured grass, dotted with short Sego palms, was a palatial building in the style of a Caribbean colonial mansion. Peach-colored with white shuttered windows and white trim, it was surrounded by tropical jungle vegetation and highlighted by golden sunshine.

The driver headed toward the circular cobblestone driveway, then stopped under the portico near the entrance, and shifted into PARK, allowing the cab to idle.

"We're here, ma'am."

"Miss," Spencer snapped, correcting his mistake.

"What?"

"I'm not a ma'am." She rolled her eyes, opening her purse to get her wallet, already deciding she wasn't giving him a tip. "I'm only twenty-three years old, which means you are to call me miss."

"Sorry about that."

"I doubt very seriously that you're truly sorry, but whatever." She gave him a dismissive wave. "How much do I owe you?"

"You don't owe me nothing," he said and then added, "Bitch."

Startled and confused, Spencer jerked her head up. Glaring at the driver, a middle-aged man with sagging, copper-colored skin, dark bushy hair, and a mole on the tip of his nose, she asked, "What the hell did you just say?"

"Cab was paid for in advance, and this is for you." He turned and tossed something at her. "On behalf of Ben Chang, welcome to Belize."

Cursing, she fumbled the small black, hard object as it fell into her lap. A cell phone. She grabbed the cell phone, stared at it, and then looked at him. "What is this?"

"Burner phone," he grunted. "Can't be traced. And here's the charger."

Another small black object sailed over the seat, this one with an electrical cord extending from the bottom of it.

"Ben Chang told you to give this to me?" she asked, heart punching as she shoved the charger into her purse. "You know Ben?"

"I work for Mr. Chang," the driver said. "He's gonna call you on that phone. Make sure it stays on. Keep it charged."

"Do you know anything about this favor he wants me to do?"

"Don't know and don't care," he grumbled. "Give me your passport."

"Give you my passport?" She glowered at him. "Are you crazy? What do you want my passport for?"

"I don't want your damn passport," he said. "Mr. Chang wants your passport."

"I'm not giving you my passport."

Cursing, the cab driver reached over the seat. Confused, Spencer shrank away from his arm, revolted by the excessive hair covering the short, stubby limb. With a snarling grunt, he grabbed the bright blue Hermes Birkin bag given to her by Rae—who'd lifted three from the closet of a "date" whose wife had about ten or twelve—and then swung it over the seat and onto his lap.

Spencer gaped at him, his audacity delaying her response for a moment before she sputtered, "What the hell are you doing?"

"I'm getting your passport."

Rising up, Spencer leaned over the seat, desperate to get the Birkin back. "Get out of my damn purse! Crazy asshole!"

The cab driver pushed her off him. She fell against the back-seat, horrified as he shoved a grimy hand into the Birkin. Rooting around in her purse, he took out her passport and then threw the purse over the seat at her. The Birkin hit her in the face.

Shrieking, Spencer tried to grab the purse as it bounced across the backseat. Grabbing the Birkin before it fell to the dirty, mud-caked floor mat, Spencer held it close to her, cradling it. "You son of a bitch! This is a fifteen-thousand-dollar purse and you pawed it with your filthy, disgusting hands!"

"Get the hell out of my cab," he said, turning away, facing the windshield.

Spencer wanted to take the Birkin and bash him over the head with it, but she didn't want to insult the purse. She forced herself to bury the anger and irritation churning within her. Why waste her rage on this jerk? Wouldn't it be better to wait and let all her ire build so she could unleash it on the person who deserved it most—Ben Chang?

Who the hell did Ben think he was? Why would he have this jackass steal her passport? Without it, she was pretty much trapped in the country. And, she supposed Ben had planned it that way. Ben wasn't going to let her leave Belize until he was good and damn ready for her to go.

Glaring at the cab driver, Spencer got out of the cab, yanking her purse and her two Louis Vuitton suitcases behind her. She had barely closed the sliding door before the man sped off, tires screeching, leaving a noxious cloud of thick, black exhaust billowing up around her. Trembling with anger, Spencer coughed, waving her hand in front of her face.

Straightening the bun she'd pulled her hair back into this morning, Spencer turned and headed into the resort, ready to get on with *Step One*.

4

San Ignacio, Belize Belizean Banyan Resort – Owner's Office

Sitting in his office, Sione Tuiali'i rubbed his jaw and stared at the stack of invoices he still needed to approve. He couldn't seem to concentrate on the invoices today. He'd been unfocused yesterday, too. The day before that, it had taken him all day to finish signing the payroll checks, a mundane task that usually took about an hour.

For too long, Sione had been ill at ease and jittery, and as much as he hated to admit it, he was wary because of the night he'd spent with a beautiful random hookup. He wasn't proud of ending up in bed with another anonymous stranger. But he didn't want to overanalyze.

Critical self-inspection usually forced him to confront truths he didn't want to acknowledge. Specifically, that he was using sex as a coping mechanism for his relationship woes.

He hadn't been looking for sex with a random girl when he'd gone out drinking with his cousins several weeks ago. That night, he'd met a girl named Kelsey Thomas who had blatantly let him know she was down for whatever, and so he'd indulged.

Another night of sex with no consequences.

Except there had been consequences.

A specific consequence named Benjamin Chang. The random hookup hadn't been random at all. The hot chick who'd come on strong had been instructed by Ben to get close to him.

Sione still didn't know why.

His attempts to get answers from Ben had ended in a violent confrontation. Whenever he was around Ben, which was rare, a lot of crazy stuff was in his head. Disgust, hatred, apprehension, and even a strange, worrisome regret.

Despite everything, Ben was like a brother to him. His uncle had once told him that he and Ben were like Cain and Abel. But who was Cain? And who was Abel? Whose blood would end up crying out from the ground?

The night he'd confronted Ben about Kelsey Thomas, Ben hadn't given him answers, but he had told him where to find them.

Ask your father.

Sione wasn't really surprised Richard Tuiali'i was behind the curtain, pulling the strings. Apparently, his father was looking for something, and that something was in Sione's casita.

Ask your father.

Sione didn't want to. Any contact with Richard was always risky.

Since their knockdown drag out weeks ago, Sione hadn't heard from Ben. Kelsey's botched attempt to find whatever Richard was looking for might have forced Ben and his father to retreat. But retreat was not a concession of defeat. Sione knew better than that. Richard was relentless when he wanted something.

And what his father wanted had to be important because Richard was never indirect or subtle. His father was all about getting what he wanted through violence and intimidation—a knife to the throat or the barrel of a revolver shoved into the mouth. The fact that his father would order Ben to find some pawn to do his dirty work was proof Richard was searching for something significant, which worried Sione.

The desk phone chimed. Relieved to be distracted, Sione was quick to press the speaker button.

"Uh, boss ... I need you, like, right now," whispered Analee, the Front Desk Assistant on duty, more than a hint of panic in her tone. "It's an emergency."

"What's the problem?"

"Irate guest."

"Where's Lenora?" he asked, thinking he would let his assistant manager deal with the irate guest.

"She had that meeting with the event planner from the bank about the convention next weekend, remember?"

Slightly irritated, Sione asked, "What's the name?"

"Edwards." Analee said. "First name, Spencer."

Sione accessed the reservation information and scanned the details. "So, what's the problem?"

"She claims she didn't book the honeymoon casita," Analee said. "She says she booked a regular casita and that's what she wants, but we don't have any regular casitas available."

Exhaling, Sione rubbed the spot between his eyebrows.

"I'm giving you fair warning, boss," Analee said. "She's a real bitch-and-a-half."

Minutes later, Sione walked out of his office and headed for the lobby. Once there, he strode to the front desk and asked Analee, "Where's the lady I need to talk to about the honeymoon casita?"

"She's over there." Analee pointed across the lobby to a cluster of couches near the wall of French doors facing the back loggia, which overlooked the pool area.

Perched on the edge of a couch was the irate guest, Spencer

Edwards. Ms. Edwards had her back to him, but from the stiff, rigid posture and the dark hair pulled back into a severe bun, he had a feeling the woman would be a handful. Reluctant, he took a breath and started toward her.

5

San Ignacio, Belize
Belizean Banyan Resort - Lobby

"Ms. Edwards?"

Behind Spencer, a nice, deep baritone floated out and wrapped around her, shaking her in a way that was slightly arousing, but she ignored the feeling.

The manager, probably, hopefully. Anxious and wondering if she could really pull off *Step One*, Spencer stood. Turning, she found herself staring up at one of the best-looking men she'd ever seen in her life, maybe the best-looking guy she'd ever seen. No, no, she wouldn't give him that much credit, but still ... he was damn good-looking, and she was flustered, disoriented, and struggling to remember why she'd demanded to see him in the first place.

"Ms. Edwards?"

"Huh," she said, chagrined at how whispery she sounded.

"I'm Sione Tuiali'i," he said. "I'm the owner and manager. How can I help you?"

"Well." She took a breath and tried not to look directly into his eyes, which were hazel and entirely too intoxicating. "You could start by giving me the regular casita I requested, not the honeymoon casita."

"I'm sorry we misunderstood your reservation." He gave her an appropriately apologetic look. "But the honeymoon casita is very beautiful."

"I'm not married." She held up her left hand, pointing at the ring finger, where there was no ring. "Why would I book the honeymoon casita when I'm not on my honeymoon?"

"Listen, how about this?" he said. "Why don't I let you take a look at the honeymoon casita? I'm sure you'll like it. It's more luxurious than a regular casita."

He gave her a smile, an enticing curve of full lips, and for some reason, she felt at ease and entranced but still a little wary.

She could tell she was becoming intrigued, but there was no time for infatuation. Not that she was really infatuated, because she wasn't. Her breathless nervousness had nothing to do with the resort manager's mesmerizing hazel eyes, or how tall and muscular he was, or the low timbre of his voice, which was giving her an unmistakable shiver in a very unmistakable place.

Mr. Tuiali'i was nice to look at, but she didn't have the time, or inclination, to drool over a good-looking man.

"Ms. Edwards?"

"How about this," Spencer countered, clearing her throat. "I'll see what I think of the honeymoon casita, and if I like it, you can give me a reduced rate."

6

San Ignacio, Belize
Belizean Banyan Resort - Honeymoon Casita

The honeymoon casita was beautiful, of course, as Spencer expected.

But all the lush, tropical flowers in various shades of fuchsia and orange festooning and adorning everything were a bit much.

In the bedroom, flowers and stems spelled out the words WELCOME across the king-sized bed. Orchid petals strewn across the floor led to the large bathroom, which was dominated by a claw-foot tub, obviously big enough for two. There were flowers on the roll of toilet paper. Flowers on the wash towels. Flowers on the soap. Flowers on every surface imaginable, even on the travertine tile in the rainforest shower.

After touring the entire casita, Spencer walked back into the large living area. Feeling a bit dejected and disgruntled, she stared at the large bottle of champagne and two glass flutes on the coffee table in the living room.

The damn place made her wish she were on a honeymoon. It made her wonder what it would be like to be Mrs. Whoever The

Hell, a new bride, in this gorgeous casita where she and her husband would make love in all five rooms. They would start in the living room, then move to the dining room and on into the kitchen, then backtrack to the bedroom, and finally, eventually, head into the bathroom to screw in the giant tub.

Clutching the burner phone, Spencer walked toward the center of the living area and sank into a chair across from the oversized couch. She reached for the champagne, and—

The burner phone rang, and she answered, forgetting about the Moet.

"Hello." Spencer jumped up from the chair and paced over toward the French doors leading out to the private terrace. "Ben?"

"Hello, sweet girl." He chuckled a little. "How are you doing?"

"How am I doing?" she asked, growing more livid, more apprehensive with each passing second. "I'm wondering why the hell you told that asshole cab driver to steal my passport?"

"I needed some assurance that you would stick around and fulfill your debt," Ben said, calmly and logically, in his deep island lilt. "I didn't want you to get any ideas about leaving Belize and flying off to some country that doesn't have an extradition treaty with the United States."

"I can't believe you did that!"

"It's depressing and frustrating, isn't it, when someone you care about steals from you," Ben said. "But eventually, I will return your passport. Unfortunately, I will never see my money or watches again."

Frustrated and pissed, Spencer said, "Okay, fine. Tell me how to fulfill my damn debt so I can get the hell out of this country! I've done *Step One*, now what?"

"Relax, sweet girl."

"Don't you tell me to relax!" She paced the length of the sofa. "Tell me what the hell the next steps are so I can get them done and get back to my life!"

"You are in no position to make demands, sweet girl," he warned. "You are lucky I'm allowing you the chance to make up for your mistakes. You are lucky I don't have you thrown in jail for grand theft larceny."

Bristling, Spencer dropped down onto the couch. There was the threat again, hanging over her head, her very own personal sword of Damocles, a warning she had to heed. She didn't like him thinking he could dictate her motives, but she was in his crosshairs because of her foolish choices.

"Don't forget I have proof that you stole from me," Ben warned. "And I don't want to get you into any trouble, sweet girl."

Spencer rolled her eyes, cursing the stupid video tape. Her image on the screen had been so clear and convincing; there was no way she could deny she was the girl taking money from the bottom drawer of the closet island.

"So, how did *Step One* go?"

"It went exactly the way you planned it," Spencer snapped. "I made a fuss about being booked in the wrong casita, and then I demanded to see the owner."

"What were your initial impressions of Sione Tuiali'i?"

Why was he asking her that? Why did he care what she thought about the resort owner? What the hell did her opinion of Mr. Tuiali'i have to do with the favor he wanted her to do?

Leery of his question, and how to answer it, she asked, "My initial impressions?"

Spencer was tempted to tell him the truth. Her initial impressions were tall, muscular, good-looking, and sexy as hell. She wanted to say I got wet just looking at him. But Ben probably wouldn't even give her the satisfaction of being jealous.

"He seemed very willing to solve the issue with the casita," she said. "I think he's going to give me the honeymoon casita at a reduced rate."

There was silence on the other end, an odd, sinister lack of sound.

Just when Spencer thought the connection had somehow been broken, Ben said, "That is rather accommodating."

"Is that what you wanted to happen?" Spencer asked. "You wanted to get the honeymoon casita at a cheaper rate, is that what *Step One* was about?"

"*Step One* was sweet girl meets the resort owner."

"Why did you have me lie about being booked in the wrong casita just so I could meet the resort owner?"

"So you could evaluate him," Ben said. "So you could determine what kind of man he is, which will help you figure out the best way to get close to him, because that's *Step Two*. Sweet girl gets close to the resort owner."

"What makes you think I can get close to him?" she stammered. "How am I supposed to do that?"

"Remember how you got close to me and tricked me into thinking you liked me just so you could get into my closet and steal from me?"

"I wasn't trying to trick you," she told him. "I did like you, Ben."

"You didn't like me enough not to steal from me, did you?" Ben asked. "You didn't like me enough to trust my feelings for you or to believe that I would have given you whatever you wanted. You didn't have to go sneaking into my closet."

Sighing, Spencer shook her head, wishing she could explain why she'd decided to "date" him. She wanted to tell him she'd stolen from him because she was afraid of his feelings and even more afraid of her own feelings. She'd been afraid she would lose herself if she fell in love with him. But would he understand that?

"So, *Step Two* is get close to the resort owner," she said, rubbing her eyes, trying not to cry. "And then what? Get into his closet and steal from him?"

"I told you the favor won't be anything criminal," Ben said, an edge in his tone. "There's no law against getting close to someone."

"Just how close do you want me to get?"

"Close, but not too close," Ben said. "When it's all over, you have to be able to walk away and not look back. You have to be able to turn your back on him, even if he's bleeding on the floor, begging you for help."

He seemed to be unable to resist trying to get under her skin, and this time, he'd gone too deep. Deeper than the knife she'd plunged into his gut.

"What happens after I get close to him?"

Spencer stood and walked to the dining area, waiting for his response, wary of what he would say to her, maybe even afraid of what he would tell her.

"I'll tell you what to do next once you complete *Step Two*."

"I need some clarification about *Step Two*," she said. "You said I need to get close to Sione Tuiali'i, but not too close. But what the hell does that mean? Why do you want me to get close to him?"

"Sweet girl, don't worry, okay?" Ben said. "I have faith in you. I know you will be able to get close enough to him."

"But not too close, right?"

"You only need to get just close enough."

Irritated, she said, "How will I know when I'm just close enough?"

"You'll know you're close enough, sweet girl," Ben said, "when the resort owner asks you out to dinner and then invites you back to his place."

Her heart slammed and she froze. The clarification of *close enough* seemed too damn much like "dating." But she didn't want to jump to conclusions. Ben had promised she wouldn't have to do anything criminal, and she had to believe him. She had to trust he hadn't lied to her.

"Once you've gotten close to him," Ben went on. "I'll give you *Step Three*."

"I don't know if I'm going to be able to get close to him." She struggled to marshal the thoughts swirling in her head. "What if I'm not his type? Maybe he doesn't trust beautiful women."

"You don't need him to trust you, sweet girl," Ben said. "And you don't need to do anything different than what you did when you tricked all those men you stole from. Just flirt with him and look pretty."

"Flirt and look pretty?" she repeated, offended by his patronizing sarcasm. "And what if that doesn't work?"

"If the resort owner doesn't respond to your beauty and false charm," Ben said, "then maybe you could sit on a park bench and pretend to cry."

His words were a sucker punch out of nowhere, right in the gut.

"Maybe that will work on him," Ben told her. "After all, it fooled me."

Spencer found it hard to breathe, found it almost impossible to recover from his verbal attack. Somehow, she found her voice and said, "I know you'll never believe this, but I wasn't trying to fool you when we first met. And I am sorry I stole from you. I know you're never going to believe that either. But maybe one day, you could find some way to forgive me."

Ben said nothing; there was only a long stretch of silence.

"Ben?" Spencer said. "Ben? Are you still there?"

Frustrated, she glanced at the phone's display.

CALL ENDED.

"Sonofabitch!" Irritated, she hurled the burner phone at the wall.

"Everything okay?"

Gasping, Spencer turned. "How did you get in here?"

"The door wasn't closed all the way," Mr. Tuiali'i said. "Are you all right?"

"Don't I look all right?" She glared at him and then went to retrieve her phone.

"Sorry, that's none of my business." Mr. Tuiali'i cleared his throat and then continued. "I may have a way to solve this problem with the casita. I don't know why there was a mix-up with the reservation."

"There was a mix-up because you hired incompetent idiots."

"I don't agree with that assessment of my employees."

"Of course, you don't." She crossed her arms. "Because then you'd have to admit you don't have sense enough to hire people who know how to get a reservation right."

"I'll give you the room at a reduced rate," he said.

"Which will be?"

"Six hundred a night."

She made a face. "Six hundred?"

"That's what you would have paid for a regular casita."

Spencer shrugged. "Guess it's the least you could do."

"I think I'm being more than fair."

"Fine." She rolled her eyes and held out her hand. "Deal."

They shook, and as he was starting to pull his hand back, his fingers closed over hers and slipped between them, becoming inexplicably entwined.

Spencer looked at him and then at their fingers, laced together, and before he could pull his hand back, she yanked hers away, frowning at him.

"Okay, well." He cleared his throat. "We've got the room rate settled."

"If there's nothing else," Spencer said, "I'd like to unpack and try to relax."

Nodding, Mr. Tuiali'i said, "Of course."

Seconds later, she slammed the door in his face. Standing in the middle of the living room, Spencer wondered if maybe she shouldn't have been so rude. After all, she was supposed to be getting close to him. The next time she saw him, she could apologize. Maybe tell him she'd had an uncomfortable plane flight. Blame her cranky attitude on economy travel. She really wouldn't be lying to him.

She'd struggled to endure two hours in a middle seat, ruminating and rehashing her mistakes, squished between a sweaty, corpulent man who snored as he slept and a hyperactive eleven-year-old who made strange beeping noises while he mumbled to himself.

Heading into the bedroom, Spencer walked into the small alcove and through the opened double-door entrance. The beautiful bedroom suite mocked her when it should have welcomed her into its tropical luxury. Like the rest of the casita, it screamed romance and love. Concepts that had thus far in Spencer's life exclusively eluded her. Romance and love had given her the cold shoulder and turned their backs on her, letting her know she wasn't good enough for either of them.

Whatever.

Wasn't as though she was interested in romance and love anyway. She wasn't interested in anything that would put her on a trajectory toward becoming "that wife."

Right now, she was interested in going for a run.

It was still light outside; the sun wouldn't go down for a few hours. A nice jog through the jungle might be good and might take the edge off. Ben's demands had her on the verge of a psychotic break. A slamming heart and labored breathing might get rid of the nervousness and anxiousness.

Running usually cleared her mind, but she had a feeling the endorphin high wouldn't banish the irritating thoughts, worries, and doubts about *Step Two*.

Getting close to Sione Tuiali'i.

Ben wanted the favor done, or else. If she couldn't do it, then what?

Spencer tried not to think about it as she walked to her suitcase. The bellman had left her carry-on on the settee at the foot of the bed, and he'd placed the full-sized one on the floor, near the bedpost.

Unzipping the Louis Vuitton luggage, she opened it. Spencer shook her head. The clothes she'd painstakingly packed were slightly jumbled. Things shifted during flight, she supposed. Digging through her clothes, Spencer searched for a pair of shorts and a tank top, wondering if—

Something came toward her, a blur of movement from nowhere. Just as she realized what it was, the opened hand crashed against her face.

7

San Ignacio, Belize
Belizean Banyan Resort

Heading away from the honeymoon casita, Sione felt off-kilter, disjointed.

But he didn't understand why. Couldn't be because of Ms. Edwards, could it? No, that didn't make sense. Usually, he wasn't rattled by a good-looking woman.

Continuing down the path, Sione forced himself to shake off the uneasiness. Probably had nothing to do with Ms. Edwards anyway. The strange feeling was most likely anxiousness about the land deal for the resort expansion. The negotiations hadn't stalled, but things weren't moving as quickly as he'd hoped.

His cell phone rang and he pulled it from his pocket.

"Sione Tuiali'i," he answered, distracted.

"It's about time you answered the phone and stopped ignoring my calls!"

Sione stopped dead in his tracks, confused, his heart slamming. Arrested by the voice, a silky, velvet purr he'd once found sexy and alluring, he stepped off the path and made his way toward a large hibiscus bush.

Cursing under his breath, he kicked himself for not checking the damn caller ID. He would have recognized the number—a woman's correctional facility in Guatemala—and then he could have ignored it and blocked it.

The last person he wanted to talk to was his damn ex-fiancée. Or, as he often thought of her, the biggest mistake he'd ever made. She had a name, but Sione didn't like to speak it aloud or even think it.

His cousins, Truman Camareno, his lawyer, and Micah Jones, Truman's bookkeeper, thought his unwillingness to say his ex-fiancée's name was some sort of indication of unresolved, undefined feelings for his ex. And his cousins were right. Somewhat.

Sione still had feelings, but they weren't unresolved or ambiguous.

There was bitterness, because her selfish choices and actions had destroyed their relationship. And regret, because he'd fallen for a lying, devious bitch. Anger, because he hadn't realized how sociopathic she was until it was too damn late. And, of course, there was guilt, because she had come to him for help, and all he'd done was make things worse for her.

"Why the hell are you calling me?" he asked.

"You have to help me get out of prison," she said. "I'm in trouble."

The demanding spite in her tone pissed him off, conjuring up all the resentment he still held toward her. Taking a deep breath, Sione focused on tempering the anger she immediately inspired.

"How did you get this number?" he asked.

A strange, muffled shriek seemed to whisper through the breeze, behind him, and he turned.

Staring at the honeymoon casita, Sione stood still, listening. What the hell had he heard? Sounded like a scream, but he wasn't sure.

And it didn't make sense.

Why would screams be coming from the honeymoon casita?

"Sione, listen to me!" she said, forcing his attention back to her. "You have to help me! I am not safe here!"

"What the hell are you talking about?" he asked. "You're not safe? What does that mean?"

"It means Richard wants me dead."

8

San Ignacio, Belize
Belizean Banyan Resort - Honeymoon Casita

Stunned, lights popping behind her eyes, Spencer stumbled. Confused and gasping, struggling to stay on her feet, she stared at the man standing in front of her, a few feet away.

Dressed in black, he was a small, wiry Asian man with sallow, pitted skin, dark eyes, and a vivid tattoo that dominated the left side of his face. Starting at his temple, the green snake coiled down the side of his cheek, under his jaw, and ended on his chin.

He sparked a memory within her, something she'd been told but hadn't believed at the time, something she refused to believe.

I wasn't aiming at you, sweet girl, I was aiming at the man behind you.

The man with the green snake tattoo.

What the hell was happening? The man with the green snake tattoo was real? No. That couldn't be true. Ben had made up that crazy story about some man who'd broken into the townhouse, hadn't he?

"Who the hell are you?" Spencer asked. "What the hell are you doing in my casita?"

The Asian man snarled.

"What do you want? Money? Jewelry?" she stammered, stalling, trying to think, to figure out what the hell was going on. "I don't have any money, but my purse is very expensive and—"

He slapped her again.

Panic exploded within her as she stumbled toward the bed. Holding a trembling hand against her stinging cheek, she fought to keep her balance.

No, a voice screamed within her. *Please, no. Not again. But somehow she knew it wouldn't matter that she was sorry. It didn't matter how hard she cried. She had done something bad, and now she was in trouble. Mama was mad. She was screaming and saying bad words.*

He clamped his hand around her arm and yanked her toward him, shaking her back to the present, far from the fear and torment that had plagued her as a child.

"Let me go!" She tried to wrestle away from him, still disturbed by the intrusive memories. "Get away from me!"

He hit her once more and then gave her a vicious shove toward the dresser.

Spencer cried out as she lost her footing and fell on the ceramic tile. Pulse pounding, she rolled over and looked up.

The Asian man stalked toward her, holding what looked like a coil of rope.

Screaming, Spencer scrambled to her feet and ran to the dresser. She grabbed the glass bowl filled with river stones, then turned, and threw it at the man. Reflexes quick, the Asian man held up a forearm, blocking the bowl, sending it in a direction away from him. Stones rained to the floor, splattering across the tile as the bowl sailed through the air. Seconds later, glass shattered against the tile.

Panicked, but refusing to give up, Spencer grabbed the bamboo vase from the dresser.

Strong fingers dug into her forearm.

"Get away from me!" She swung her free arm toward the

Asian man, slamming the vase against the side of his head, leaving a bloody scratch across his cheek.

"Bitch!" The man pressed fingers against the wound and then slapped her with the rope clutched in his other hand, sending her stumbling. Crying out, realizing she was free from his grip, she used haphazard momentum to stagger to the phone on the night table beside the bed. Hands trembling, she yanked the receiver from the base.

The Asian man grabbed her wrist and forced her to face him. Grunting and cursing, he tried to wrestle the receiver away from her. Spencer fought to maintain possession but felt her fingers slipping. With only one hand, the man yanked her wrist back and forth, and her body followed, as though she was a rag doll, but she prayed for strength. And courage. And the wisdom to figure out how to get away from this crazy son of a bitch. The rope terrified her. She couldn't let him tie her up and take her somewhere to do God only knew what the hell kind of torture he had planned for her.

He pushed her to the floor. Struggling to her knees, Spencer grabbed the phone receiver she'd dropped and hurled it at him.

"Bitch!" He ducked and then kicked her, his foot connecting with her shoulder.

Screaming, Spencer went down on her hip. The Asian man reached an arm toward her.

"No! Get away from me!" She scooted back against the tile. "Stay away from me!" She thrust the heel of her foot into his groin.

As he cried out, grabbing himself, Spencer scurried to her hands and knees and then staggered to her feet. Eyes on the row of French doors on the opposite side of the room, she jumped onto the bed, crawled across the duvet, and scrambled off the other side. Feet slapping the cool tile, she ran to the doors leading out to the terrace.

Grabbing the doorknobs, she twisted and yanked, desperate to escape. The doors didn't budge. Panic exploded within her. Abandoning the knobs, she beat her fists against the glass panes. "Help me! Please somebody help me!" She banged harder but knew it was no use. No one was going to hear her scream. No one was going to come running to her rescue.

No one had ever come when she was a little girl. She'd had to endure the pain and horror. She always had to suffer being slapped, shoved into walls, being kicked, and cursed at, because she'd done something wrong.

This time would be no different. Swallowing her tears, Spencer turned.

The Asian man leaped at her.

9

"Richard wants you dead?" Sione asked, wondering why the hell he didn't just hang up on the crazy bitch. "Really? Well, if that's true, and I don't think it is, then you are in trouble. So, good luck."

He didn't have time to deal with her today—or tomorrow either. Or, even the next day. Never was when he would have time for her. He was more interested in the strange noise he'd heard. Had it been a scream? Maybe the cry of a wounded animal?

"*Good luck?*" She seethed. "I tell you that your psychotic, sadistic father wants to kill me, and you wish me good luck."

"What the hell am I supposed to do?" he asked. "Give a damn that Richard wants you dead?"

"You should give a damn about that promise you made to me," she said. "That promise you broke. You said you would help me, but you didn't. And now I'm going to die in this damn hell-hole because of your stupid mistakes."

The rabid accusation in her voice should have enraged him, but he sensed his anger dissipating as the guilt flared again. He couldn't understand why the hell he felt so responsible for the mess she'd gotten herself into? His ex-fiancée was in prison because of her choices, not decisions Sione had tricked her into making. The prison sentence was her punishment for trusting the wrong man.

Sione had been brutally honest with her. He'd warned her about Ben Chang, and had told her how Ben treated women he supposedly gave a damn about. Ben would find out all her secrets and the weaknesses and flaws she tried to hide. Then he would use those flaws against her, for his benefit and to her detriment. Once she was no longer useful to him, Ben would destroy her life.

His ex-fiancée hadn't listened to him. She was in that damn Guatemalan hellhole because of her mistakes, not because of the mistakes Sione had made when he'd tried to help her two years ago. Sometimes, he felt compelled to make up for those past mistakes, but not today. Not when she was obviously grasping at straws, trying to use his animosity toward his father to goad him into paying attention to her plight.

"Why does Richard want you dead?" Sione asked.

"Six months ago, your father came to visit me in prison. He wanted me to steal something from Ben Chang. I told him no. Your father doesn't like it when people tell him no," she said. "Now, he wants me dead because—"

"How is this my problem?"

"You have to tell Richard not to hurt me!"

"My father and I don't speak."

"Your father will listen to you!" she said. "You know Richard will do anything for you! Please! You have to help me! You can't let your father have me killed!"

Sione grabbed the back of his neck and tried to massage away the tension in his muscles. He wanted to be pissed, but the desperation creeping into her tone bothered him. And the trace of fear he heard beneath the desperation made him pity her. "Let me think about it," he said. "I'll get back to you."

"Sione, wait!" she said. "Don't hang—"

A shrill shout split the thick, tropical air. Startled, he dropped his phone, staring toward the honeymoon casita. A scream, no doubt about it. But why?

Another ear-splitting wail burst forth, followed by the screech of spooked birds.

Sione took off, forgetting his phone and the call from his ex-fiancée.

10

San Ignacio, Belize
Belizean Banyan Resort - Honeymoon Casita

Screaming, Spencer tried to dodge the Asian man's grasp, but he was too quick. Grabbing her arm, he manhandled her toward the bed.

"Let me go!" She struggled, slapping at him with her free hand, scratching at his face.

Despite her efforts, he wrestled her onto the bed. Terrified of being raped, she fought harder, hitting and kneeing and clawing, wild and chaotic in her attack. Survival instincts took over, removing all precision or organization from her assault.

He slapped her and then forced her over onto her stomach. Her face pressed against the thick, plush bed linens, Spencer struggled to breathe as she felt the Asian man's knees on either side of her hips. He yanked her right arm behind her back, his rough movements causing her torso to lift, and she was able to turn her head, exposing her face to the air she desperately needed. Taking several deep breaths, she felt her left arm join her right.

Fighting dread and tears, Spencer winced as the man wound thin straw rope around her wrists. "Why are you doing this?" she asked, grimacing from the fine bristles, like needles against her skin. "What are you going to do to me?"

The Asian man pulled the rope tighter.

"You're the man who broke into Ben's townhouse, aren't you?" she asked, trying to distract him with questions, hoping to buy herself some time to think of how to get away.

"No more talking, bitch," the Asian man said.

"Ben told me about you," Spencer said, twisting her neck to look over her shoulder at him. "Why did you break into his house?"

Scowling, the Asian man said, "Shut up bitch, before I—"

The Asian man cried out, a hint of surprise in the high-pitched screech. Less than a second later, Spencer watched, utterly confused, as the Asian man seemed to fly back away from her.

11

San Ignacio, Belize
Belizean Banyan Resort - Honeymoon Casita

Sione squeezed the back of the man's neck as he pulled the asshole away from Ms. Edwards. Dragging him to the foot of the bed, Sione stepped back when the man rolled over the suitcase on the settee and hit the floor. Struggling to manage his rage and confusion, Sione stared at the man.

A small, thin Asian guy with tight, lean muscles and a bizarre green snake tattooed on his face. Who the hell was this son of a bitch? What the hell was happening? Why had he been straddling Ms. Edwards and tying her hands behind her back? How the hell had he gotten into the honeymoon casita?

The Asian man tried to scramble to his feet, but Sione kicked him in the side. Yelping in pain, the man rolled over onto his stomach. Sione bent down and yanked the Asian man to his feet. Moaning, the man held a shaking hand in front of his face as his knees buckled. Still holding him by the throat, Sione forced the man to stay on his feet.

He wanted to crack the son of a bitch in the jaw and then

listen for the sound of bone breaking, the way Richard had taught him. *Don't stop until you hear that crunch.*

His father's vicious, chilling instructions. Lessons Sione had tried to forget, but never really could. Right now, he didn't want to forget. The man's rough assault of Ms. Edwards was a direct threat to everything he valued and worked hard to maintain, everything he tried so damn hard to convince people he deserved. The son of a bitch couldn't get away with attacking one of the resort's guests.

Letting the rage have its way was something he couldn't do, though. He had to control the anger. But, it was difficult, and all he received for his efforts to stay calm and collected was frustration, multiplying within him, taking over his senses, the rational part of him.

A sensible response was too much to ask at the moment.

Quickly and without much reluctance, Sione reverted to the way he'd been taught to deal with cowardly assholes and crashed his fist into the center of the man's face. There was no crunch of bone, but it was still a knockout punch. Sione pushed the man away, disgusted with himself for following his father's example instead of handling things the way his uncle had taught him.

Groaning, the Asian guy stumbled as he sidestepped into the wardrobe and then collapsed in a heap. Sione glared at the man, sprawled on the floor, his face already swollen and purple.

"Oh my God! Is he dead?"

Sione turned to look at Ms. Edwards. Sitting in the middle of the bed, she looked beautiful and tempting despite her disheveled appearance. Wisps of hair had escaped the severe bun at the back of her head, and her breasts rose and fell at a tantalizing pace beneath a slight tear in the neckline of her clingy dress. With her mouth slightly parted and the sultry scowl enhancing her delicate features, he felt the rage dissipating, turning to lust.

San Ignacio, Belize
Belizean Banyan Resort - Honeymoon Casita

"Are you deaf?" Spencer asked, rolling over onto her hip and then rising to her knees. "Did you kill him?"

The resort owner faced her and took a step toward the bed. Gasping softly, Spencer stared at him, trying to summon up a bit of shock. Maybe some outrage. She needed something to combat the disturbing, inappropriate feelings snaking through her, feelings of lust, which had started several moments ago, when she'd turned over onto her back and sat up just in time to see Sione Tuiali'i smash his fist into the Asian man's face.

The resort owner's attack had been savage, and yet there was something hypnotic and enticing about the brutality he'd displayed. His aggressive ferocity was both violent and sexy. Despite herself, she'd been turned on by the idea of the hands he'd used to hit the Asian man caressing her nipples, trailing along the surface of her skin as they moved past her navel and then lower, slipping between her—

"Are you okay?" the resort owner asked, concern in his hazel stare.

"Am I okay?" She rolled her eyes. "Did you really just ask me that?"

"Can you tell me what happened?"

"It's obvious what happened to me!" she said. "A crazy asshole broke into my casita and tried to kill me! The question is not *what* happened. The question is *why* did it happen? How was some psycho able to break into my casita? I thought this resort was safe!"

"It is safe—"

"The website said this resort was a relaxing and safe tropical oasis in the jungle—"

"Relaxing, safe rainforest sanctuary," he corrected.

"Whatever," she said through gritted teeth. "The point is, your website lied. Relaxing and safe, my ass. I don't know what the hell kind of place you're running, but in case you didn't notice, I am not relaxed, and I do not feel safe!"

"Ms. Edwards, I am very sorry that this happened to you," he said. "And I want you to know that I will do whatever I have to, whatever it takes, to make sure you're okay and you enjoy the rest of your stay. After I call the police, I am going to meet with my security team—"

"Your security team?" she scoffed. "Is that a joke? A security team is supposed to make you feel secure, and I have never felt more unsecure in my life!"

"I am going to find out how that man was able to get into your casita," he continued. "But, rest assured, he won't get a second chance to hurt you again."

"Well, of course, he won't," she said. "Because you killed him. Dead men don't attack helpless women!"

"He's not dead."

"Are you sure?" she asked. "You beat the hell out of him."

"Because he was assaulting you," he said, frowning. "I was trying to stop him from hurting you."

"What is it?" Spencer asked, wary of his searching gaze, the way those hazel eyes seemed to roam over her body, almost as tangible as if he was touching her. "Why are you staring at me?"

"Your tone," he said, the corner of his mouth lifting slightly.

"What about my tone?" she asked, unable to tell if his gaze held amusement or derision.

"It's a bit ungrateful," the resort owner said. "More than a bit, actually."

"Ungrateful? Excuse me?" She gaped at him, trying to move her wrists beneath the rope. "I am not ungrateful! I am petrified! I was viciously attacked! And then I was calf-wrestled and tied up like a heifer! God knows where that asshole planned to take me or what he was going to do to me when we got there! So, excuse me if I don't seem grateful enough for you!"

"Ms. Edwards, I'm sorry," he said, holding up both hands. "You're right. You've been through a lot. I shouldn't have accused you of not being thankful that I saved your life."

"You saved my life?" She glared at him. "Is that what you think?"

"What I think, Ms. Edwards," he said, "is that if I hadn't come in here when I did, there's no telling what that guy would have done to you."

"Oh, so now you think you're some kind of hero? Well, let me tell you something," she said. "I didn't need you to come in here and go all jungle warrior on him for me, okay? I was handling the situation!"

"And while you were handling the situation," he said, walking away from the bed. "You somehow got your hands tied behind your back?"

Spencer scooted to the foot of the bed.

"What the hell happened to the phone?" he asked, glancing

back at her and then at the floor, where the house phone lay in pieces, wires strewn across the tile.

"When I was handling the situation," Spencer said. "I threw the phone at the guy."

The resort owner sighed and then said, "I'll be back."

"What? Where are you going?" Alarmed, Spencer made her way off the bed, mindful of the river stones as she stepped on the tile.

"I need to call the police, but I think I dropped my phone outside. So, I'll have to use the one in the kitchen because you broke this phone."

"I didn't break the phone!" Offended, she said, "I was trying to defend myself. The damn phone ended up broken because he ducked out of the way at the last minute."

Shaking his head, the resort owner headed out of the bedroom.

"Come back here!" she said. "You need to untie me!"

"You sure you need my help?" he said over his shoulder, walking out of the bedroom. "Don't want you to think I'm trying to be a hero. Wouldn't want you to accuse me of not letting you handle the situation."

Frustrated and flummoxed, she stayed on his heels as he headed into the living room.

"Considering that I was almost killed on your property," she said, "I think you should be a little bit more considerate of me and my feelings and what I had to endure!"

Sione Tuiali'i stopped abruptly.

Squealing, Spencer skidded, unable to stop her momentum, and crashed into the resort owner's back. Taking a step back, she overcompensated, lost her footing, and cried out as she teetered backward and—

He turned and grabbed her, steadying her so she wouldn't fall on her ass. His fingers wrapped around her arms gave her a surprising jolt of pleasure. Disturbed by her response to his touch, she stared ahead and found herself eye level with his massive, muscled chest.

"I'm sorry," he said. "You're right. You've been through a very traumatizing situation, and I need to be more sympathetic and understanding. Again, I'm very sorry, and I hope you'll accept my apology."

"I'll think about accepting your apology," she said, adopting a sassy tone, even though his sincerity was evident. "After you untie me."

San Ignacio, Belize
Belizean Banyan Resort - Honeymoon Casita

Deciding not to antagonize Ms. Edwards any further, Sione bit his tongue. He would forget about the comeback he wanted to sting her with, which would have been something about not wanting to untie her. She looked good with her hands tied behind her back, defenseless and helpless. He could do what he wanted to her, and she wouldn't be able to get away.

He supposed she wouldn't have appreciated his mocking, and he would have been treated to more of her insolent attitude. Her bitchiness should have irritated him, but he rather liked the boldness. It brought out the sultriness he found so intriguing. Her annoyance held a hint of self-reliance, which suggested she had no time for vengeance or carrying grudges. He had the feeling she wouldn't hold his earlier lack of sympathy toward her plight against him.

Sione hadn't meant to act as though he didn't care, because he did. The safety and well-being of his guests was the most important thing to him. When he'd seen the Asian guy tying her up, he'd had no problems giving into his anger to make sure nothing bad happened to her.

He would have done the same for any of his guests. For whatever reason though, she'd accused him of trying to run to her rescue and be a hero instead of being glad he'd saved her. The ungrateful attitude had reminded him of his ex-fiancée. He didn't have time for another woman making him feel as though helping her was the least he could do.

The entitlement in Ms. Edwards' tone and demeanor made him feel as though what he'd done deserved no applause. Not that he was even looking for effusive gratitude, because he wasn't. He didn't want Ms. Edwards to gush over him and thank him profusely for rescuing her, but he didn't want her to bitch at him for saving her life either.

He untied her, disturbed by the welts and abrasions on her wrists from the rope burns.

"Thank you," she said, careful as she pressed a finger against her wrist.

"There should be a first aid kit in the kitchen," he said, guiding her to the dining room table. He pulled a chair out, and after she sat down, he went to the kitchen. Returning to the table, he removed a small plastic bottle and several cotton balls from the kit.

"Tell me what happened," he said, reaching for her hand.

"What are you going to do?" she asked, trying to pull her hand away.

"Just going to clean the wounds."

"Is it going to sting?"

"I don't think so," he said. "It's peroxide."

Her gaze wary, she allowed him to pull her hand closer to him.

"Now, tell me what happened," he said, soaking a cotton ball with peroxide.

"The guy broke into the casita," she said and then winced

when he pressed the cotton ball against her wrist. "And he attacked me."

"You didn't see him breaking into the casita?"

"I was unpacking," she said, making another face as he dabbed the cotton ball across the abrasions on her skin. "And then I turned around, and the next thing I knew, I was slapped in the face."

Sione winced. The idea of her being slapped in the face rekindled his anger, and for a moment, he wished he'd broken the guy's neck. But when the wish lasted longer than a moment, he struggled to combat the violent thoughts. "Did he say anything to you?"

"Anything like what?"

"Did he give you any indication as to why he broke into the casita?" he asked. "Was he trying to rob you? Or was there something in the casita he wanted? Or—"

"I think he was, um, trying to rob me," she said. "Because he wanted my purse."

"Your purse?"

Nodding, she said, "It's Hermes. Vintage. Worth about twenty thousand."

"A twenty-thousand-dollar purse?" he echoed, staring at her, shocked, but not really surprised. She looked like the kind of woman who liked expensive things; her beauty was a suitable match for luxury goods, but something in her gaze made him doubt her ability to afford high-dollar trinkets.

"Why did he tie you up?" he asked. "If he wanted the purse, why didn't he just shove you aside, take the purse, and get out as quick as possible?"

"How the hell would I know what goes on in the mind of a psychotic purse snatcher?" she asked. "Maybe he tied me up because I fought him. I wasn't going to let him take my purse. My sister gave it to me, and she went through a lot to get it."

"Still seems strange."

"What seems strange?"

"Going through the trouble to tie you up," Sione said.

"Maybe that's his thing," Spencer said. "Maybe he likes to tie women up before he snatches their purses. I don't know. Like I said—"

There was a loud, abrupt slam.

"What the hell?" Sione jumped up from the table and headed toward the bedroom.

Moments later, in the master suite, he stared at the empty space on the floor in front of the bamboo-wood wardrobe, and he couldn't help but remember something else his father had always told him.

Don't ever assume a man is down for good. Make sure he won't ever get up again.

"What is it?" Ms. Edwards asked.

"Damn it," he mumbled, turning to her. "The son of a bitch is gone."

———

Want to keep reading?

Buy your copy of Flawless Danger today!

EXCLUSIVE OFFER FROM RACHEL WOODS

Rachel Woods has been entertaining readers with her brand of romantic suspense -- sexy dangerous fiction. Now you can get one of her books for FREE, you just need to go to the link and tell her where to send it: http://eepurl.com/bxtIF9

In addition to the FREE book, you'll also get:

- Access to Rachel's Flash Fiction for FREE, exclusive to her mailing list subscribers.
- Chance to win books and Amazon gift cards in Rachel's monthly giveaways.
- Invitation to join Rachel's advance readers team — Sexy Dangerous Partners.

What are you waiting for? Join today!

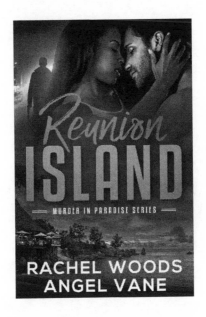

ABOUT THE AUTHOR

Rachel Woods studied journalism and graduated from the University of Houston where she published articles in the Daily Cougar. She is a legal assistant by day and a freelance writer and blogger with a penchant for melodrama by night. Many of her stories take place on the islands, which she has visited around the world. Rachel resides in Houston, Texas with her three sock monkeys.

For more information:

www.therachelwoods.com

therachelwoodsauthor@gmail.com

ABOUT THE PUBLISHER

BONZAIMOON BOOKS

BonzaiMoon Books is a family-run, artisanal publishing company created in the summer of 2014. We publish works of fiction in various genres. Our passion and focus is working with authors who write the books you want to read, and giving those authors the opportunity to have more direct input in the publishing of their work.

To receive special offers, bonus content and news about our latest ebooks, sign up for our mailing list on our website.

For more information:
www.bonzaimoonbooks.com
bonzaimoon@gmail.com